Keys to Wonderlust

Kimber Guise

First Edition

This is a work of fiction.

Names, characters, businesses, places, events, locales, and incidents are either the products of the author's imagination or used in a fictitious manner. Any resemblance to actual persons, living or dead, or actual events is purely coincidental.

Table of Contents

Chapter 1:
The Pink Slip and the Package

Haylee felt it in her gut before her manager ever spoke.

Eighteen years in accounting—faithful, efficient, invisible. She'd skipped birthdays, worked through migraines, and volunteered for weekend inventory audits no one else would touch. All of it had earned her a beige envelope with her name typed in the corner and the phrase, "We're making difficult decisions." Just like that, it was over. No farewell party. No gold watch. Just a box of her things and a stunned walk through the rain-slicked parking lot, a plastic plant jutting out of the top like an accusation.

The office had never meant much—just gray cubicles and flickering fluorescents—but it had been her world. Nearly two decades balancing numbers, reviewing statements, and sitting through meetings that blurred together in a beige haze. At some point, pride had given way to survival.

When her boss called her in that morning, she knew. The tight jaw, the folder already on the desk, the careful sympathy in his voice.

"Haylee, I wish I had better news…"

She barely heard the rest. Words like restructuring and severance buzzed around her like static.

She nodded, packed up her things, and walked out into the gray afternoon. It wasn't just a job she lost. It was the scaffolding of a life she wasn't even sure she believed in anymore.

Later That Evening

The house was too quiet. The kind of quiet that pressed on your chest. Haylee wandered the living room, straightening cushions and picking up her empty coffee mug. Everything felt dulled, like someone had turned the color saturation down on her life. She paused at the bookshelf. Her fingers drifted over the dusty spines of novels she'd always meant to read. There had never been time. Always another deadline, another report, another task that mattered more than she did.

The front door creaked open. Jake's footsteps echoed on the hardwood.
"Hey," he called, tossing his keys on the counter. "How was work?" She turned slowly. Her voice came quieter than she expected. "I got laid off today." He paused just long enough to make it awkward, then shrugged off his jacket.

"Damn. That sucks. You'll bounce back, though. You always do."
He flopped onto the couch, grabbing the TV remote. Haylee stared at him. This was the man she'd spent ten years with—the one who'd made her laugh in college, who never remembered the dishes but always brought home the right wine. Now, he just felt like furniture.

She poured herself a glass of that same wine—red, cheap, necessary—and sat at the kitchen table, staring at the floor. "What do you want to do about dinner? Are you making something, or should we
order in?" he called. He didn't ask how she felt.
Didn't even look up.

She felt a pit open in her stomach. Why couldn't he just be there for her, just once?

"I guess I'll order pizza again," she murmured.

"Sounds great. Just... no mushrooms this time, okay?"

She grabbed her phone and opened the DoorDash app.

The Package

The next morning, a package arrived—real mail, with a handwritten return address in loopy cursive: Aunt Aggie.

But Aunt Aggie had died two weeks ago.

Haylee opened it slowly. A faint lilac scent drifted from the folds of the paper. Inside was a letter, dated three months earlier:

Haylee-girl,

If you're reading this, I'm gone—but don't be sad, okay? Life isn't meant to be tied up in office chairs and shared bank accounts.

I left you something. Actually, a few things. Check with my friends, Marla and Benny, at Happy Pines RV Park. They've got Bertha's keys and a few boxes of memories.

And remember that crystal ring I gave you in college? You might need it more now than ever.

Take care of yourself the way I couldn't. And maybe—just maybe—you'll remember who you used to be.

Love, Aunt Aggie

A VHS tape slid from the envelope and hit the floor with a soft clack. Haylee blinked. Who even played these anymore?

Later that week, she got the call about the will. Aunt Aggie had left her a truck, a beat-up RV named Bertha, a stack of photo albums, and a cedar-scented leather journal filled with cryptic quotes and scribbled margins.

Jake's response?

"A truck and an RV? Seriously? What are you gonna do with that—camp in your feelings?"

He laughed, but Haylee didn't.

Something about the tape, the letter, the scent of lilac and cedar—it stirred something. A memory, maybe. A possibility.

She called her father. They hadn't spoken properly in years, not since her mother's funeral.

"She left you Bertha?" he said, a surprised chuckle in his voice. "Your aunt was always full of surprises. You know she once drove that RV through Mexico with just a dog and a ukulele?"

"I didn't know that."

"There's a lot you didn't know about Agnes," he said softly.

"And maybe a lot you've forgotten about yourself."

The Choice

That night, Jake didn't ask how she was feeling. He talked over her silence.

"I mean, it's not like they fired you for screwing up," he said from the couch.

"You're smart. You'll bounce back. This isn't the end of the world, Hay."

She sat across the room, wine glass in hand. "It kind of feels like it."

He laughed like she was being dramatic. "You always get like this when something goes wrong. You overthink everything. This is just... a reset."

She didn't respond.

He paused his game, finally looking at her. "You're not seriously thinking about keeping that RV, are you?"

"I don't know. Maybe. It's what Aunt Aggie wanted."

Jake snorted. "Yeah, but Aggie wasn't exactly... grounded. Sweet lady, sure, but she lived in a fantasy world. No offense, but chasing her ghost across the country won't fix your life."

Her grip on the glass tightened.

"You've got responsibilities," he added. "Rent. Bills. We have plans. You can't just toss that out for some dusty RV and old photos."

"We haven't made real plans in years, Jake."

He looked confused. "What are you talking about? We've got a good setup. I work from home, I cover the utilities, you handle the rest. We're a team."

A team. That's what he called it. She called it stagnation.

Jake leaned forward, voice softening. "Look, I get it. You just lost your job. You're freaking out. But this isn't the time to do something reckless."

She blinked. "Reckless?"

"Yeah. Selling everything, driving off in an RV to find yourself? That's not you. That's Instagram crap. Hashtag freedom. You're smarter than that."

There it was.

The quiet little cage he always built around her—made of logic, practicality, and words that sounded like love but felt like limits.

"I think I need some space," she said.

Jake shook his head. "No, you need stability. You're not twenty-five, Hay. You don't get to run."

"I'm not running," she said. "I'm waking up."

He rolled his eyes. "You really think this RV thing is going to fix you? That's what this is, right? You're bored or unhappy or whatever, and now you want to blow up your life because your weird aunt left you a nostalgia-mobile?" She stood slowly. "I've spent too long letting someone else decide what my life should look like."

She walked to the bedroom door, Bertha's keys in her hand. Behind her, Jake sat with his headset on, half-lost in another round of digital warfare. "You're really doing this?" he called, voice sharp. "You're gonna throw everything away? For what—some dead woman's fantasy?" Haylee turned back. "She wasn't just some woman. She lived more in a month than I've let myself live in ten years." He stood, eyes narrowing. "So that's it? After everything we've been through, you're just walking out?" A flicker of guilt sparked in her chest, familiar and reflexive. He was good at that— twisting the story until she felt like the villain. Like she owed him her silence. "I supported you," he added. "I was patient. While you worked late, buried yourself in spreadsheets. And now, when things go sideways, you run?" She hesitated. What if he was right? What if this was just a breakdown in disguise? Then she remembered something—Aunt Aggie's voice on that grainy old VHS. She'd watched it earlier that day, hunched over the only thrift-store player she could find. The footage was shaky, but Aggie's eyes sparkled under a desert sun, wind whipping through her hair. "Stop waiting for permission," Aggie had said. "No one ever gives it. You just have to take the damn road." Haylee blinked back tears. That woman—the one with the sun in her eyes and dust on her boots—that's who she wanted to be. Not the version Jake kept chained to comfort.

She looked at him one last time. "You were never patient. You were just in control."
He opened his mouth to reply, but she was already stepping into the bedroom.
She didn't slam the door.
She didn't need to. Some endings
don't need punctuation.

He laughed—cold this time. "You're gonna regret this."

She didn't answer. She just walked to the front door and slipped Bertha's keys into her coat pocket. Her necklace came off next, the crystal ring catching the porch light as she paused at the door.

Jake didn't follow.

"Unbelievable," he muttered, turning the game back on.

She didn't make a scene.

She just walked out, lungs full of night air and a strange, stubborn kind of hope.

She didn't know exactly where she was going.

But for the first time in a long time, she knew she was finally going somewhere.

Chapter 2:
Bertha at Happy Pines

Happy Pines RV Park wasn't all that happy.

It sat just off a forgotten stretch of two-lane highway, wedged between a shuttered ice cream stand and a faded gas station with one working pump. A crooked line of mailboxes leaned like old men waiting to share secrets. But when Haylee pulled her borrowed sedan into the gravel lot, something about the place tugged at her chest.

Maybe it was the towering pine trees, whispering in the breeze. Or maybe it was the hand-painted wooden sign nailed to a rusting post, the turquoise paint peeling:

Come as you are. Leave better.

She hadn't told Jake she was going. He would've twisted it into an argument, made her feel guilty, called it reckless or selfish. Not that he'd even noticed she was gone. Probably thought she was still sulking in the bedroom.

Haylee parked beside a sun-bleached trailer and stepped out into the warm, pine-scented air. A woman in leopard-print leggings and garden clogs approached, her smile wide and welcoming.

"You must be Haylee," she said, pulling her into a hug that smelled of cinnamon gum and dryer sheets. "I'm Marla. That lug over there's Benny."

A tall, balding man in a Hawaiian shirt waved from a porch swing.

"You were so little the last time we saw you," Marla beamed. "Aggie talked about you like you were her own. She loved you, something fierce."

Haylee's smile faltered. *Like you were her own.* People said things like that, but something in Marla's voice made it feel heavier. She filed the words away without knowing why.

"She left you a treasure, that's for sure," Benny said, nodding toward the back lot. "Bertha's in Spot 27. Been waiting on you."

Ber tha.

8

Haylee followed them around the corner, her sneakers crunching on gravel until they reached a crooked pine tree shading an even more crooked RV.

Bertha wasn't pretty.

The RV's beige siding was cracked and sun-faded, its awning hung like a dislocated arm, and the windows were cloudy with grime. Still, Haylee stood in front of it, heart pounding, a strange warmth rising up her spine.

It felt like stepping into a memory she hadn't known she still carried.

When she opened the door and stepped inside, she was instantly ten years old again. The scent of patchouli clung to the curtains. A stack of photo albums sat neatly on the booth dinette beside a worn leather journal. A tiny TV was mounted above the windshield, its VHS player blinking 12:00.

Aggie's energy was everywhere.

Benny handed her a manila envelope. "Your aunt prepaid the lot for a month. Said she had a feeling you'd come."

Haylee turned the envelope over in her hands. Inside were registration papers, a spare key, and a folded note written in Aggie's messy scrawl:

There's more than one kind of inheritance, Haylee-girl.
This is the kind that gives back when you use it. Not when you sell it.
Don't let the fear talk louder than the wonder.
Love you always,
—Aunt Aggie

That night, Haylee curled up on the narrow bed at the back of the RV, her old tourmaline ring nestled in her palm. She didn't sleep well. The wind creaked through the trees, and every groan of the RV felt like it was remembering something. But when morning came and sunlight spilled through the dusty blinds, she didn't wake with dread.

For the first time in months, she didn't want to crawl back into herself.

She made coffee with a travel kettle Marla had loaned her and sat on Bertha's steps, the leather journal open in her lap.

The first entry was dated fifteen years ago.

If you're reading this, I'm probably off chasing something stupid and beautiful.
Remember, Haylee: the world is too big to live in one place forever.
Take risks. Fall in love with the journey, not the destination.
And never apologize for wanting more.

Haylee closed the journal, her heart pounding.
Aggie had always known. Even then.

The Next Morning

Despite everything, Haylee drove to her father's. The weight of unanswered questions settled heavily in her chest.

Inside, it was the same—quiet, stagnant, lined with dust and memory. Her father sat at the table, shuffling papers. He didn't look up.

"Morning," he said, flat.

"Mor ning."

He pushed a stack of documents across the table. "Agnes left the truck and RV to you. You should go through it all when you have time. Most of it's probably junk."

Haylee didn't respond. She wasn't sure what she felt.

"I'm thinking about keeping it," she said after a pause. "Just for a while. To figure some things out. I need space."

He didn't argue. His voice came quieter this time.

"You've got space here."

"Not the kind I need."

As Haylee lingered by the door, she noticed a photo tacked to the fridge—one she'd never paid attention to before. Aggie, holding baby Haylee in a sunlit field. Her expression was full of joy, fierce and soft all at once.

A chill pricked her skin.

For a long moment, he stared at her—really stared. Then he stood, walked to the fridge, and pulled down the photograph.

"Before you go," he said, handing it to her. "Agnes always said this was her favorite. I kept it on the fridge for years."

Haylee took it.
Agnes, holding her in a field. Both laughing, radiant, whole.
It hit her like a wave.

"Always meant to be together," her dad murmured.

The words cracked something open.

That Evening

Back at Happy Pines, Haylee sat cross-legged on Bertha's floor, surrounded by her aunt's things. The scent of patchouli and aged paper hung thick in the air as she sifted through photo albums, letters, and old Polaroids.

Aggie's life unfolded in fragments—sun-soaked road trips, dusty festivals, cryptic journal entries. Every item was a whisper, a breadcrumb trail leading somewhere Haylee hadn't dared to go.

She picked up a photo: Aggie beside a gleaming, younger Bertha, smiling wide beneath a desert sky. The RV had once looked full of promise. Now it was weathered and worn—like she had lived a thousand lives inside it.

She opened another journal. The pages were soft with wear.

If you're reading this, I'm probably off on another adventure.
I'm not one for settling down—you know that.
You don't have to have all the answers yet, Haylee. That's the beauty of it.

The words sank deep.

Somewhere between a job she hated and a relationship that had chipped away at her confidence, Haylee had forgotten she used to dream of more.
Aggie had lived freely, fiercely.
Haylee had traded that for predictability, for someone else's version of "enough."

The RV didn't feel quite so foreign now.
It felt lived-in. Loved. Waiting.

She didn't know what the road ahead looked like.
But for the first time in a long time, she wanted to find out.

Chapter 3:
The Road Ahead

Haylee stood outside Bertha, the low morning sun casting soft golden hues across the pine trees that stood like quiet sentinels around the RV. The stillness of the air was almost reverent, broken only by the occasional rustle of branches or birdsong calling across the clearing. The place felt strangely alive this morning—less like an artifact from her aunt's past and more like a starting point for her own.

She wrapped her arms around herself, not from the cold—it was already warming up—but from something else. Something inside that was beginning to shift. It had been years since she'd allowed herself to dream. To want something just for herself. She had always followed the path laid out for her—first the career she didn't love, then the relationship that slowly suffocated her. Day after day had passed in a blur of obligation, duty, and quiet resignation.

But now, with the weight of Aggie's passing and the unexpected inheritance of this weathered, wandering home, she had something she hadn't felt in a long time: *a choice.*

Bertha, with her faded beige siding and sagging awning, had become more than just an old vehicle. She was a symbol—of motion, of escape, of possibility. The chipped paint, the dusty windows, the stickers from places Haylee had never been —they spoke of a life lived boldly. Aggie had chased joy like it was her job. She'd believed in detours, in broken plans, in following the sun.

Haylee took a slow step forward and placed her hand against the RV's doorframe. "What were you thinking, Aggie?" she whispered, her breath catching. "Why me?"

She stepped inside. The air was thick with memory. The familiar scent of patchouli and stale incense clung to the walls, instantly pulling her back to childhood. It was as if she were a kid again, curled up in the corner while Aggie made tea over a sputtering little stove, telling tales of border towns and desert skies, wild coincidences and unexpected kindnesses. There had always been magic in her aunt's stories—magic Haylee had grown up believing in, then slowly forgotten.

She ran her fingers over the worn leather seat cushions, soft and sun-faded. The fabric still held the shape of someone who had lived here fully, completely. On the table sat Aggie's journal. Haylee picked it up, her thumb tracing the creases in the worn cover before flipping through the pages. Bits of Aggie's life spilled out in loops of ink—scraps of poetry, musings, moments frozen in time.

She stopped at a page that seemed to leap out at her:
I don't know how long I'll be in this place, but it feels right. I'm finding things I didn't know I was looking for. There's freedom in every choice, and that's all we ever need.

The words hit her like a punch to the chest. Her breath caught, tears threatening at the corners of her eyes. Aggie had always known. She hadn't just said things to sound wise—she had meant them, lived them. Haylee had been going through the motions, tethered to expectations she didn't remember agreeing to.

And now... she didn't have to be.

She let the journal fall shut and rested her hand over it for a moment. Then her phone buzzed in her pocket.

She didn't want to check it.

Her dad had already left a message earlier about the estate, about "finalizing things." She wasn't ready to face that—not while everything else inside her still felt so unsteady.

Another buzz.
Dad: *Lawyer said we need to finalize the estate soon. Don't drag this out.*

The message was short, to the point—like always. Her father had a way of reducing complex, emotional moments to tasks to be completed. He didn't mean to be cold, but that was how it always felt. He moved forward like nothing could— or should—slow him down.

She stared at the message, her fingers tightening around the phone. The expectation in it was heavy. She could already picture the conversations ahead: logistics, numbers, forms. As if Aggie's life, her essence, could be boxed up and processed like any other transaction.

She set the phone down on the counter and let out a breath that felt like it had been trapped for years.

She didn't know what she wanted. Not yet. But she knew she couldn't keep existing in this haze, tiptoeing around everyone else's comfort. Something had to change.

The map app was still open from the night before—an old habit she'd picked up from Aggie's stories.

16

Whenever she felt stuck, she'd pull out a map and pick somewhere to go, even if it was just the next town over. Movement, she had said, was sometimes the only cure for a heavy heart.

Haylee studied the screen. The nearest town, small and tucked between hills she'd once driven past but never stopped in, blinked up at her like an invitation.

She didn't have a plan. But maybe she didn't need one.

A sudden knock at the door startled her.

She stood quickly and opened it to find Marla, one of the longtime residents of the park, standing there with a basket of muffins and a warm, knowing smile.

"You up for some company?" Marla asked.

Haylee hesitated for just a second, then nodded.
"Sure. Thanks."

Marla stepped inside, casting an affectionate glance around the RV.
"Aggie sure loved this," she said. Her gaze settled on the journal and photo albums on the table. "She always said Bertha was her true home. That she found herself out on the road. I think she left it all to you because she knew—you'd need it."
"You really think she knew?" Haylee blinked.

"I do," Marla said softly. "Aggie wasn't the type to leave things to chance. She saw you. Even when you didn't see yourself."

Haylee sat down, her fingers brushing the corner of a photo album.
"She was so full of life," she said, voice barely above a whisper. "I don't know if I'm ready for all of this."

"No one ever is, sweetheart," Marla said as she placed the muffin basket on the dinette. "But that's never stopped the world from spinning, has it? You're here.

You're thinking about what's next. That's how it begins."

Haylee let the words hang in the air. She didn't know what "next" looked like. But she was beginning to believe that maybe, just maybe, she could find out.

Marla gave her a soft pat on the shoulder and stood.
"Take it one day at a time. Let Bertha speak to you. She'll tell you what you need to know."

After she left, the RV felt different. Quieter, yes—but not hollow. It felt like it was waiting. Like Aggie was still here, somehow, cheering her on from just beyond the veil.

Her phone buzzed again.

Another message from her dad.

She let it go unread.

Instead, she pulled up the map again. Her hand hovered over the keys in the ignition.

Maybe it wasn't a huge leap. Maybe it wasn't running away.
Maybe it was just... starting.

And maybe that was enough.

She turned over the key.

Bertha rumbled to life beneath her, the engine's low growl vibrating through her feet and into her bones.

And Haylee, still full of questions but no longer frozen by them, shifted into gear. She didn't know exactly where the road would take her.

But for the first time in a long while, she was finally moving forward.

Chapter 4:
The Crystal Ring

The crystal ring had once meant everything to Haylee.
Now, it hung on a thin silver chain around her neck, resting over her heart like a forgotten promise.

She hadn't taken it off since the funeral. Truthfully, she hadn't even wanted to go. She'd spent most of the service feeling like a fraud, surrounded by people who had stayed close to Aggie in the years Haylee had been too busy—or too self-involved —to write, call, or visit.

College had swallowed her whole. Then the job. Then Jake.
There were so many excuses. Too many.
She hadn't been a good niece. She hadn't made time for the one person who had always made time for her.
And now Aggie is gone.

The last time Haylee had seen her aunt clearly was her sophomore year. She'd come home for spring break, angry at everything—herself, her parents, her life—rushing around, anxious to be anywhere but home. Aggie had made her tea, a ritual of comfort that never failed to calm her. And then, she handed her a small velvet box.
.

"I want you to have this," Aggie said, eyes warm with something Haylee hadn't recognized then. "It's black tourmaline. Protection, grounding. You're gonna need it."

Haylee had laughed—awkward, dismissive. "You and your crystals, Aunt Aggie."

Aggie hadn't been offended. She'd only smiled and pressed the box into her hands.

"You don't have to believe in it. Just wear it when you forget who you are."

Haylee hadn't understood. Not then. She'd tucked the ring away in a drawer, forgotten like most gifts from people who saw her better than she saw herself.

Now, the weight of it against her chest felt like an anchor—like a thread leading her back to something she hadn't even realized was missing.

She sat at Bertha's dinette, Aggie's journal open across her lap. She had been avoiding it for days, afraid of what it might stir. But now, the quiet hum of the RV park and the gentle ache behind her ribs pushed her to listen.

The journal was a mosaic of Aggie's life—scraps of memory stitched together in ink and margin notes. Lists. Quotes. Doodles. Recipes. A pressed four-leaf clover, yellowing with age.

Entries stretched across decades:
"Snowed in at Zion. Made chili in a pressure cooker that nearly exploded. Worth it."
Met a woman named Tilda who swears she fought a mountain lion with a tent pole. I believe her."
"Still think about Haylee. Wonder if she's happy. Wonder if she remembers the creek."

The creek.

Haylee pressed the page to her chest and shut her eyes, letting the memory bloom. A sliver of forest behind Aggie's old cabin. Muddy toes, laughter, the scent of pine and woodsmoke. They used to run barefoot, pretend to be witches with moss in their hair. Aggie had shown her how to build a fire, how to watch the wind, and how to trust her instincts.

"You're magic," Aggie had said once, the words steady, absolute. "Don't ever let anyone dim it."

Back then, Haylee had let those words wash over her without sinking in.

Life got too loud, too full. College applications. Internships. Rent. Jake.
She didn't have time to be magic.
She didn't have time to be herself.
But now, sitting in this faded RV, the ring heavy around her neck, she needed to remember.

She stood and walked barefoot to the tiny bathroom. The cracked mirror reflected someone she barely recognized. Pale. Distant. Like a shadow of herself.

She lifted the chain over her head and slipped the ring off, holding it under the flickering light. The black tourmaline gleamed—glossy and jagged, beautiful in its imperfection. The silver band was slightly warped, its edges worn smooth by time.

"I'm still here," she whispered to her reflection.

But even as the words left her mouth, doubt hovered.
Was she?

Her phone buzzed from the counter. Jake.
She didn't even hesitate this time. She silenced it, opened the cabinet, and shoved the phone deep inside.

Outside, Benny's laugh echoed across the park. Tools clinked. Birds called to each other from the treetops. The wind moved like a song through the branches.

The Road to the Past

The drive to the RV park felt longer than it should have. It was only a few miles outside of town, but each curve in the road pulled Haylee deeper into the past. The pavement stretched ahead like a question she didn't know how to answer. Was she heading toward something better—or simply running from the life she no longer wanted?

The truck's engine hummed, steady and low. Inside her chest, her thoughts were anything but.
She gripped the steering wheel tighter, knuckles pale.

She had lost her job. Let go of the life she'd spent years building. And now, she was about to face something even more daunting: Bertha. Her aunt's RV. Her aunt's legacy. Her aunt's freedom.

Haylee had promised herself she would never settle. But somehow, in between career moves and compromise, that's exactly what she'd done.

A job that drained her.
A relationship that dulled her.
A house that echoed with everything unsaid.

Now, she had a chance to start over. If she was brave enough to take it.

As the truck rolled to a stop at the RV park entrance, her pulse picked up. The sun was dipping low, casting a golden glow across rows of trailers and campers. The whole place felt suspended in a kind of quiet magic—unassuming but oddly comforting. Like the world was holding its breath just for her.

She stepped out into the pine-scented air and let it fill her lungs. It was a strange blend of calm and fear—like standing on the edge of something that could change you if you let it.

The park itself was modest. Gravel paths. A scattering of trees. A small office by the entrance where a few people lingered.

It wasn't flashy. But it had a presence. Soul.

Bertha was parked under a cluster of trees ahead, looking more weathered than she remembered. Chipped paint. Rust. A little sag in the awning. But even still, something about it felt like home.

She walked slowly toward the RV, heart thudding in her chest. Her hand hovered over the door handle for a beat, then pulled it open.

A rush of air met her—musty and still—but layered with something comforting. The faint scent of sage and cedar.
A scent that wrapped around her like a memory.

Inside, the RV was cramped but cozy. Faded cushions, old curtains, sunlight filtering through streaked windows. A life paused mid-sentence.

Postcards covered the walls. Trinkets lined the shelves. A journal lay open on the counter, waiting.

As her fingers brushed across familiar objects, a flicker of warmth bloomed in her chest. This was Aggie's world. Unpolished. Wild. Honest.

Could she learn to live this way? Could she really let go of everything she thought she was supposed to want?

A knock at the door pulled her back.

She turned just as it creaked open. A woman stood there with a large binder and an easy smile.

"Hi, I'm Sarah," she said. "I helped your aunt around here. I think we met once, a long time ago."

Haylee blinked, trying to place her. "Right. Sarah. I'm... Haylee. I'm just trying to figure it all out."

Sarah chuckled. "That's how most people start. Your aunt would've wanted you to feel at home here. Don't rush anything. Just take it one step at a time."

Haylee's shoulders eased. "Thank you. I appreciate that. I don't really know where to begin."

"You don't need to. Aggie never had a plan, either. She just lived." Sarah's eyes softened. "She always said it wasn't about the RV. It was about freedom. About remembering who you are."

The words lodged deep in Haylee's chest.

She had spent years just surviving. Doing what was expected. Checking boxes.
But living?
That felt foreign.

"Would you like me to show you around the park?" Sarah asked. "We can grab coffee after, if you want. I've got a few good stories—and tips about RV life."

Haylee hesitated, then smiled. "Sure. I'd like that."

As Sarah walked away, her footsteps crunching down the gravel path, Haylee lingered in the doorway, watching the sun dip lower through the trees. The RV park was peaceful in a way that made her chest ache.

She hadn't known how much she needed quiet. Space to hear herself again.

Her hand rested on the doorframe. The rough wood beneath her fingers felt solid, g rounding.

For a moment, she considered calling Jake. Telling him everything. But then she remembered his last message, his careless tone, his ability to make her feel like too much—or never enough.

She shut her phone off and slipped it deep into her purse.

If she was going to rediscover herself, she couldn't do it by reaching back to people who only wanted the version of her that stayed small.

She stepped barefoot into the open space ahead. Gravel bit her feet. The sky was gold and soft. The world felt wide.
She breathed.

The journal called to her again. She glanced back through the RV window at it, pages slightly curled. Aggie hadn't waited for permission to live. She didn't need all the answers.
And maybe Haylee didn't either.

The Breaking Point

Bertha sat under the tall pines like a relic of something sacred. Sun-bleached and rusted, she wasn't much to look at—but standing before her now, Haylee felt a pull. Like the RV had been waiting for her all along.

Jake showed up three days later—uninvited, unannounced, and holding two coffees from the overpriced café downtown like he deserved a medal. He leaned against the truck door like he was posing for an ad: smug, arms crossed, sunglasses on despite the overcast sky.

"I figured I'd come see what all the hype was about," he said, a faint smirk tugging at his lips.

Haylee blinked at him, the RV door halfway open behind her. "You didn't respond when I said I needed space."

"You didn't say you were moving into a tin can in the woods."

"It's an RV park," she said flatly. "And I'm renovating it."

Jake offered her a coffee. "Okay, but like—what's the plan, Hay? You gonna live in this thing? Drive around like some digital nomad hippie? Where are your benefits? Your routine?"

She didn't take the coffee.

"Aggie left it to me. There's a reason."

"This is what your aunt left you?" he said, incredulous. "I thought it'd be... newer. It's basically a tin can."

Haylee didn't answer. She stepped inside.

The scent of sage and cedar was immediate—her aunt's presence still lingering in the fabric of the space.

On the dinette table: a thick journal, some VHS tapes, a photo album tied with twine. A crystal dangled in the window, spinning slowly in the light.

She opened the journal. On the inside cover, her aunt's handwriting:
"Haylee, if you're reading this, you're ready. Or maybe just tired of waiting. Either way—go. Live. Don't wait for permission."

Her throat tightened.

Behind her, Jake sighed loudly. "Seriously? You're not actually thinking of keeping this thing."

She didn't turn around. "I'm not sure yet."

Jake climbed in after her, surveying the RV like it was beneath him. "Even if we fixed it, it's too small. Where would I stream? There's no space. Barely a desk."

"I never said you had to come," Haylee replied, calm but firm.

Jake's head snapped toward her. "What's that supposed to mean?"

"I need space. Time. I'm thinking about staying here for a while. Maybe six months. Maybe longer."

He laughed—cold, dismissive. "Six months? So what—you're quitting life to go off the grid? Just like that?"

"I already lost my job, remember?" Her voice cracked, then steadied. "And maybe I need to lose a few more things to find what matters."

Jake threw up his hands. "So this is it? You're having some spiritual crisis over your aunt's dusty stuff and now you're becoming a full van-life influencer?"

Haylee met his eyes—quiet. Resolute.

"It's not dusty stuff. It's her life. A life that mattered. A life that had meaning."

27

He rolled his eyes. "You can't even change a tire, Haylee. You think you're going to just... hit the road and become some bohemian wilderness guru?"

"I'll learn."

"Or you could be rational," he snapped. "Sell this thing. Use the money for something responsible. Something that actually builds a future."

Her fingers curled around the counter's edge.

"A future, like what?" she asked, voice low. "Like ours? You glued to your screen, me killing myself to keep everything running? I've been surviving, Jake. Barely. And I'm done."

His face hardened. "So that's it. You've been waiting for a reason to leave."

She stepped forward, locking eyes with him. "No. I've been waiting to remember who I am. And I think I just did."

Jake folded his arms, posture rigid. "Fine. Run away. Just don't expect me to be here when you fall apart."

Haylee watched him glance around the RV, unimpressed. She could already see the critique forming: the unfinished flooring, the half-painted cabinets, the dust on the fan blades.

He sat on the dinette bench, tapping the table with his fingers, posture laced with judgment. "You can't be serious about this. I mean, I get it—grief makes people impulsive. But come on, babe. Sell the RV, get a little apartment, regroup. We'll figure things out."

"We?" she echoed, voice tinged with disbelief.

"You don't really want to start over at thirty-six, Haylee. Not really. You had a stable job, a house, a relationship—"

"With someone who hasn't picked up a dish in four years," she snapped.
That shut him up.

Jake leaned back, sighing like he was the one exhausted. "You're not being fair."

"I've been fair for ten years," she said, her voice sharp. "I've been quiet. I've been small, tired, and reasonable. And guess what it got me? A pink slip and a boyfriend who's more in love with his Twitch stream than with me."

Jake rubbed his forehead, like she was the problem to solve. "So what—now you're just gonna leave? Drive off in this thing with no plan? That's not you."

"You don't know who I am anymore," she said, her voice hardening. "And honestly? Neither did I—until I got here."

His tone shifted, softer now. Vulnerable. Reaching. "Hay. You're just spiraling. This is you being scared."

"No," she said sharply, stepping back. Her hand gripped the crystal ring beneath her shirt like a lifeline. "Stop calling me Hay. It's Haylee. And this is me being done."

Aunt Aggie's journal sat open beside her. One page read:
"There's nothing braver than walking away from what no longer resonates."

Jake followed her gaze and scoffed. "She was always filling your head with that mystical crap. That's not real life."

Haylee looked at him—really looked. And for the first time, she felt nothing. No anger. No longing. Just the kind of clarity that settles seconds before sunrise.

"I sold you the house and the car, Jake," she said, quiet but firm. "I gave you everything you asked for. Let me go."

29

He opened his mouth, then closed it again. The words had nowhere to land.

Finally, he nodded—slow, reluctant.

"Whatever. Have fun finding yourself or whatever. You'll be back."

She watched him walk back to his car. His footsteps faded. The taillights disappeared down the winding road out of Happy Pines.

And in the silence that followed, something unknotted inside her.

It wasn't grief. It wasn't fear.
It was freedom.

She stepped outside. The trees swayed gently overhead. The world stood still, as if holding its breath.

She had no map. No clear plan.
But the weight in her chest had shifted.

She wasn't just walking away from him—
She was walking toward something.

And the crystal at her throat caught the last rays of light like a compass.

Chapter 5:
The Escape

Haylee didn't cry until she was on the road.

Bertha groaned and creaked behind the wheel, but she was moving—slow, steady, and stubborn, like something alive. The ignition had turned over without hesitation, and something about that felt like a sign, as if Aggie herself were saying, It's time, Haylee.

She had no plan. Just a one-month paid lot at the RV park where her aunt had lived. No backup. No income. No house anymore—Jake was buying out her share.

But for the first time in years, Haylee felt light.

The RV park came into view, nestled behind a stand of trees like a secret waiting to be discovered. The air was thick with pine and earth—the scent of homecoming. She parked awkwardly in a gravel slot, Bertha's wheels kicking up tiny clouds of dust as she came to a stop. Her legs shook as she stepped out. Her chest tightened. She inhaled deeply.

The enormity of what she'd done hit in waves.
She'd left him. Left the house. Left everything behind.

And she wasn't sorry.

A cheerful voice cut through her thoughts. "Hey there, you must be Haylee!"

A woman approached, her smile wide and welcoming. Early sixties, sunflower-patterned maxi dress, Birkenstocks. Her name tag read **Mavis**.

"I knew your aunt," Mavis said warmly. "She was a legend around here."

Haylee tried to smile. Her voice cracked. "I just... I need a minute."

Mavis' expression softened. "Take all the minutes you need. When you're ready, there's a potluck at seven. No pressure. Just good food and good people."

Haylee nodded, watching her walk away before turning back toward Bertha.

The air was golden. Still.

The pines rustled gently overhead, and for the first time since leaving the life she'd known, she felt... **free**.

New Beginnings, New Faces

Haylee woke to birdsong.

She hadn't realized how much she'd missed nature until now. The air felt different here—cleaner, brighter, like every breath was clearing away years of mental dust. She stretched, rolling out of bed, still adjusting to the idea of calling Bertha home.

Her aunt's RV wasn't fancy, but it had a quiet charm. Yesterday she'd unpacked what little she'd brought, adding pieces of herself: journals and photographs on the counter, a stack of favorite books in the corner, candles on the shelves.
The space felt lived-in. Loved.

After a quick breakfast of cereal and coffee, she decided to explore.

The sun greeted her as she stepped outside. Gravel crunched underfoot as she walked past rows of RVs, each with its own personality—some sleek and modern, others sun-faded and patched with care.
This wasn't just a park.
It was a community.

She spotted Mavis by a picnic table, chatting with a man adjusting solar panels on his roof. Haylee approached, nerves fluttering but hopeful.

"Good morning!" Mavis called. "This is Greg—one of our longtime residents. He's the solar expert around here. If you ever want to go off-grid, he's your guy."

Greg looked up and grinned, wiping grease-streaked hands on a rag. Mid-forties, sun-creased face, kind eyes.

"Nice to meet you, Haylee," he said. "Mavis says you're new to all this. Don't worry—it's not as scary as it seems."

"Thanks," Haylee said, easing into the moment. "I've got a lot to learn, but I'm looking forward to it."

"Well," Greg chuckled, "the first thing to know is that everything takes a little more effort on the road. But it's worth it. If you ever need help—plumbing, power, anything—you know where to find me."

"Thanks, I really appreciate that."

They chatted a bit longer before Greg returned to his work. Haylee felt a flicker of relief.
The people here were kind. Present.
The vibe was open, inviting.
Nothing like her old life, where even close friends had started to feel far away.

As she wandered, she noticed little touches of personality scattered through the park: vegetable gardens in repurposed crates, hammocks swinging lazily under tall trees, wind chimes singing in the breeze. One RV had strings of colored lights wrapped around its awning. Another had a *"Free Herbs"* sign stuck into a pot of basil.

It was peaceful.
Real.
And it felt like something she hadn't dared to believe in for a long time: *home.*

Around noon, Mavis found her again.

"Hey, the potluck's starting in about an hour," she said, smiling. "You should come. Great way to meet people. No pressure—we don't do pressure here."

Haylee hesitated.
Mingling with strangers still felt like walking into cold water.
But she reminded herself: this was why she came.
To start again.

"Okay," she said with a small smile. "I'll be there."

Later That Evening; The Potluck

The communal space was nothing fancy—just a small open-air structure with picnic tables, a fire pit, and mismatched chairs. But the warmth from the fire and the smell of grilled food made it feel like home.

A dozen or so RVers had gathered around, chatting and laughing, swapping stories like old friends.

Mavis introduced Haylee to a few people, including Linda and Rick—full-time RVers for nearly fifteen years. Their rig was old but full of character, like them. "When we started," Linda said, "we didn't have a clue what we were doing. But you learn. It's about being flexible—changing plans when life throws you something better."

Rick nodded. "And the people you meet? Worth every flat tire and detour."

Haylee smiled. Their stories were like Aggie's—full of freedom, grit, and moments that mattered. It was nothing like her old life, where routine had dulled her sense of wonder.

After dinner, the fire cracked and popped as conversations meandered. Someone strummed a guitar. Someone else passed around homemade cookies.
Haylee listened, laughed, and, for the first time in a long time, belonged.

She wandered the park again later, wrapped in that afterglow of good food and genuine company. The RVs, scattered but grounded, felt more like homes than any suburban cul-de-sac she'd known. Each had a life, a story, a soul.

Gardens grew in pots and bins. Wind chimes sang. A couple swayed in a hammock, their laughter like wind in the trees. A woman with silver hair knit peacefully in a rocking chair. A man strummed quiet folk songs beside a flickering lantern.

It was simple.
Beautiful.

Here, no one was rushing.

No one was selling a version of success.

People lived slowly, intentionally. They helped each other without keeping score.

Haylee could feel it—that quiet freedom, that space to just be.

She hadn't realized how lonely she'd been until she wasn't anymore.

She still didn't know what came next.

Chapter 6:
The Same Kind of Crazy

Bertha creaked as she settled, the sounds of metal and wood shifting like a sigh. Haylee curled into the dinette-turned-reading-nook, her aunt's journal resting on her knees. The scent of lavender and old ink lingered on the pages like a memory. Her aunt's looping cursive captured desert sunrises, strangers-turned-family, and long nights under star-choked skies.

It was all so alive.
And it made Haylee ache.

She traced the faded ink with her fingers before closing the journal and pressing it to her chest. Outside the small window, golden light filtered through the pines. In the center of the park, flames danced in the fire pit again. Laughter floated on the breeze. Another potluck. But before she could join them, she had to make one call.

Her stomach tightened as she picked up the phone.
Dad.

He hadn't called about the RV. Hadn't asked. She wasn't surprised. Her father had always hidden his emotions behind practicality—especially after losing her mom and Aunt Aggie.

Three rings.

"Haylee?" came his voice—gruff, cautious.

"Hi, Dad. You busy?"

"Just watching the game. What's up?"

She twisted the crystal ring around her neck. "I wanted to tell you something. About the RV."

A pause. "You're selling it?"

"No," she said, steadying her breath. "I've moved into it. I'm at Aggie's old park. I'm renovating it. Maybe traveling. Trying to figure things out."

The silence stretched, only broken by muffled sounds of the game in the background.

"You're serious?"

"I am. I've been lost for a long time. The job, Jake—none of it made me happy. This feels different. It feels like mine."

A sharp exhale. "You sound just like her."

"Like Aggie?"

"Yeah," he said, too quickly. "Wandering around in a tin can. No plan. No stability. No sense. Your mother and I worked hard to give you a real life."

"I know," Haylee said quietly. "And I followed all the rules. Got the job. Bought the house. Stayed with the wrong person. But I was miserable."

"Happy?" he scoffed. "Life isn't about being happy every damn minute. You think Agnes was happy when her alternator blew out in Wyoming? When she couldn't pay taxes?"

"She lived on her own terms," Haylee said, pulse rising. "She lived, Dad. And she left something that actually feels like me. That matters."

A pause. Then: "You're chasing a fantasy, kiddo. That's not how the world works." Her throat tightened. "I called because I hoped you'd be proud."

"Haylee—"

"But instead, you just want me to stay small. Like you. Like Mom did."
"That's not fair."

"No, what's not fair is being made to feel crazy for wanting more. Aggie wasn't afraid to live. If that makes me crazy, then I'm proud to be the same kind of crazy."

Silence.

She didn't wait for a response.
Haylee hung up and set the phone beside her.
The silence in its wake felt cavernous—but oddly peaceful. Outside, laughter and guitar chords floated through the trees. A dog barked. Leaves rustled like a slow exhale.

She stood, smoothed her sweater, and grabbed a mason jar of lemonade from the fridg e.

She wasn't broken.
She was just becoming.
And right now, that was enough.

Later That Week: Demo Day

The next morning, Haylee stood in the center of Bertha with a crowbar in hand and a hundred doubts crawling across her chest. The RV looked even smaller now that she was about to rip it apart.

"Start with the carpet," Benny had told her. "If you hate it, you can't ruin it."

So she did.

The passenger-side chair went first—bolted down with rust and defiance. Then the stained beige carpet, layered with dust, glitter, and stories that weren't hers. The subfloor beneath looked tired, but solid.

Kind of like her.

She was mid-pry on the kitchenette faucet when gravel crunched outside. A truck door slammed.

Then: "Still got all your fingers?"

She froze.

Her dad stepped through the door, toolbox in one hand, a six-pack of lime seltzers in the other.

"Don't get excited," he said, handing her pliers. "I'm mostly here to supervise and tell you what you're doing wrong."

She offered a crooked smile.

He didn't smile back, but he didn't leave either.

They worked quietly, side by side. Pulled down old wallpaper. Uncovered a faded sunflower mural Aggie had painted.

"She always loved those damn flowers," her dad said, softer now. "Your mom did too."

They kept working. Awkward silences filled with effort, stories, and a few jokes that almost landed. It wasn't healing. But it was a beginning.

By sundown, the washer/dryer was halfway installed.

"Insulate the pipes," her dad said before heading out. "You'll freeze your butt off in the fall."

That night, Haylee sat cross-legged in a pile of tile boxes and crumpled sketches. Aggie's journal lay open beside her. Her eyes caught a familiar line:

If I die before Haylee sees this: remind her she's tougher than she thinks.

Tears welled, but she didn't cry.

This wasn't just a renovation.
It was a reclamation—of space, of self.

And for the first time in her adult life, Haylee wasn't trying to prove she was okay. She just was.

The Days That Followed

She didn't sleep much that night. Every creak of Bertha's bones reminded her how temporary this life was—but also how alive it felt. The silence here wasn't heavy. It was open.

She kept replaying her dad's voice. Fear. That she'd end up like Aggie—scraping by, rootless. But she had also been free. Brave.

Maybe Haylee could be, too.

The next morning, she made coffee on the tiny stove, steam curling into the cool air. She sketched layout ideas on a cereal box: reading nook, herb garden, extra storage. She wasn't building a checklist for a life anymore—she was building one from the inside out.

A knock at the door startled her.

Marla stood there with a tray of muffins and a thermos of spiced tea.

"I figured you might not have a full kitchen yet," she said with a grin. "And people think better with carbs."

They sat on the RV steps, sipping tea and watching birds in the trees. Haylee asked about Aggie—how she was, why she chose this life.

Marla spoke of thunderstorms and barefoot dancing. Of tears during sad movies. Of fierce, unconditional love.

"I think Aggie always knew she wouldn't grow old the traditional way," Marla said. "But she wasn't afraid. She made peace with being the same kind of crazy."

Haylee laughed through a lump in her throat. "She made it look so easy."

"It wasn't. But it was worth it. And so will you."

The Work Continues

That afternoon, Haylee jumped back into the project. FaceTimed Benny about solar. YouTubed RV plumbing tutorials. Made a supply run. Chose a peel-and-stick tile that looks like aged wood. Yanked out a dinette bench to build a cozy nook with pillows and a faux fireplace.

Marla gasped when she stopped by again.

"She'd be so proud."

"I hope so."

"You're making it yours. That's the point."

Not everything came easily. One night, trying to install a backup camera, Haylee had a quiet meltdown over a missing screwdriver. No tears. Just stillness. A slow unraveling of exhaustion and self-doubt.

Her phone buzzed—a friend suggesting a job and writing, "When you're ready to get back on track…"

Back on track.
As if this wasn't one.

Maybe they were right.
Or maybe—for the first time—Haylee wasn't falling apart.

Chapter 7:
The Tape and the Treasure Hunt

Haylee found the camcorder while digging through the last of the plastic bins Aggie's friends had stashed in Bertha's dusty under-compartment. It was wedged between a box labeled Maps & Misadventures and an old flannel shirt that still smelled like Lavender, campfire, and a thousand desert nights.

The camcorder was scratched but sturdy—a chunky early-2000s model with a flip-out screen and a mini VHS cassette still inside. Her heart skipped. A sliver of Aggie's voice? A breadcrumb? She hovered over the power button.

The screen flickered—then died with a sad little beep. Battery dead. No charger in sight.

"No, no, no," she muttered, turning Bertha inside out like a woman possessed. Cabinets, glove boxes, bins, even the storage spaces under Bertha—nothing. Benny's universal charger didn't fit. Marla tried to help and offered a blender cord "just in case." Her dad chuckled when she asked if he had a camcorder.

"Haylee, I barely own socks without holes. Try Facebook or a garage sale."

So she did.

The first Marketplace seller ghosted her. The second agreed to meet in the parking lot of a bowling alley, where a woman with pink hair, a fanny pack, and strong fairy godmother energy handed her a dusty camcorder, said, "God bless you, sweet soul," and vanished into a neon-lit Uber like a wizard.

Back at Bertha, Haylee held the tape in her hands. It felt ancient. Sacred. Jake had once rolled his eyes at tapes like this, calling them "obsolete." But now, it was something else—a whisper from the past. A tether to a woman who never did anything halfway.

She slid the tape into the camcorder, hands trembling.

Static. Then—Aggie.

Her aunt appeared on the tiny TV screen, cross-legged on Bertha's original couch, hair tied in a blue bandana, eyes twinkling like she'd just shared a secret with the stars.

"Hey, Haylee-girl. If you're watching this, I've probably gone and joined the stardust by now."

Haylee gasped softly. The voice. The familiar tilt of Aggie's head. It was like she was still alive and laughing just down the road.

"Don't freak out about the RV. I know it's a mess. But so were we once, and look how we turned out."

The video cut to a tour: Aggie pointing at pipes and wires, waving like a magician-slash-mechanic.

"Don't dump your black tank in flip-flops. Rookie mistake. And check your propane line before lighting anything, unless you like flying."

She thumped the AC unit. "If it freezes, pull the filter and rinse it under hot water. Easy peasy."

And then, with a smirk: *"Never trust a man who says he doesn't know how to do laundry. He's lying, baby girl."*

Haylee laughed, tears falling freely now.

This wasn't just an instructional video. It was Aggie leaving her courage in a bottle. A practical love letter. A cosmic pat on the back.

The tape ended with Aggie holding a small leather notebook.

"Keep a log. Write everything down. Where you go. What you eat. Who you meet. Make your life your own damn story."

Then she looked straight into the lens
.

"I love you, kid. Now go live."

The screen went blue.

Haylee sat in the still glow of the small screen, the air charged with the aftershock of love. Slowly, she stood, crossed to the glove box—and there it was. The very notebook. Worn brown leather, soft with age.

The first page was blank.
The second had a single sentence in Aggie's looping scrawl:

"Don't let the world write you small."

Firelight and Fails

That night, Haylee walked down to the firepit with a mason jar of lemonade and a nervous knot in her stomach. The RV park's communal space—little more than a gravel circle wrapped in string lights—buzzed with laughter, food, and the sizzle of something being heroically overcooked on a portable grill.

A crooked banner stretched between two trees:
Wander & Wonder: Potluck Night

Haylee lingered on the edge until a voice called out, "New girl!"

She froze.

A wiry old man with a Gandalf beard and suspenders waddled over, balancing a paper plate stacked dangerously high with baked beans.

"You must be Aggie's niece."

"Yeah," Haylee said, trying not to laugh. "I'm Haylee."

"I'm Buck. I live in the old school bus with a cactus on top. Don't eat Marlene's casserole unless you're ready to see your past lives."

"Marlene!" Buck hollered over his shoulder. "I'm warning the civilian!"

Marlene—tie-dye hoodie, galaxy leggings—flipped him off and waved sweetly at Haylee.

"Welcome, honey!"

More names followed in a blur of kind eyes and wonderfully strange stories:

Terry and Lou, who traveled with a tiny goat named *Disco.*

Jasmine, a solar-powered van lifer and vlogger.

Bryce, a former lawyer turned potter who said stress melted out of him like clay.

Lenny, who made candles in a converted delivery truck and whispered existential truths when you least expected it.

It felt like she'd stepped into a sitcom called The Misfits of Lot 17.
And for once, she didn't want to leave.

Later That Night

After too much food and cider punch with probably more than "a splash" of moonshine, Haylee climbed into Bertha to use her own bathroom for the first time.

She flipped the switch for the water pump.
Nothing.

No hum. No lights. Just Bertha sitting there, fully dead and utterly unbothered.

Panic rose. She fumbled with breakers. Jiggled wires like that ever helped. Whispered desperate apologies to whatever RV gods she might've offended.

Then—knock knock.

"Need a hand?" Buck's voice floated through the dark. "Sounds like your battery disconnect tripped. Or you insulted the fuse gods."

She opened the door, sheepish. "I might've plugged in a slow cooker."

"Welcome to RV life," he said, flipping a hidden switch in the electrical bay.

The hum returned. Lights blinked on. Haylee could've hugged him.

"Thanks."

He winked. "Just wait 'til your black tank backs up. That's the real baptism."

Open Mic Surprise

Back at the firepit, tiki torches flickered and someone—probably Jasmine—had set up a tiny amp.

"Open mic night," Marlene announced. "Wasn't planned. Never is."

Jasmine crooned Fleetwood Mac.
Lou read a poem about goats and galaxies.
Bryce did slam poetry about cubicles and printer jams.

Then someone nudged Haylee.

"Your turn," Jasmine said, offering her a spot by the fire.

She hesitated, then ran back to Bertha, grabbed Aggie's journal, and returned to the circle.

"I didn't write this," she said, voice soft. "But I think it still belongs to me."

She read aloud:

"Some nights, the loneliness feels like a mountain I'll never climb. But then I light a candle, boil some tea, and remember—freedom is the price I chose. And it's worth it. Even on the cold nights. Especially then."

Silence.
Then warm, steady applause.

Haylee exhaled a breath she didn't know she was holding.
For the first time in a long time, she didn't just feel like she belonged.
She felt seen.

The Unlikely Mentor

The next morning, Haylee sat outside Bertha with a mug of coffee and Aggie's journal on her lap. The park was quiet—birds chirping, a distant generator humming. She was still thinking about Aggie's tape. Her words. The notebook. The firelight.

Jasmine approached, coffee in hand.

"Mind if I join you?"

"Not at all," Haylee said, gesturing to the folding chair beside her.

Jasmine had been one of the first to welcome her, offering help with solar hookups and boondocking tips. They'd shared laughs, stories, even awkward silence that somehow felt comforting.

"I've been thinking," Jasmine began. "We all come here for different reasons. But we end up teaching each other things along the way."

Haylee nodded. "It's like... our stories intersect. And that intersection becomes the lesson."

"Exactly," Jasmine said with a grin. "And sometimes, the best lessons come from the most unlikely places."

They talked about the upcoming community showcase. Jasmine planned to sing. Haylee, now inspired, decided she'd read something of her own.

As the event drew closer, the two spent more time together—trading stories, fears, bits of hard-earned wisdom. Jasmine's philosophy—freedom over fear, presence over perfection—began to settle deep in Haylee's bones.

The night of the talent showcase, everyone gathered around the fire again. Jasmine's song was raw, soulful. When it was Haylee's turn, she stood up, journal in hand, voice steady.

She told her story.

Not the cleaned-up version. The real one. Loss. Discovery. Fear. Choice. And what it meant to start again, even in her thirties.

When she finished, the applause wasn't just polite—it was heartfelt.

Afterward, Jasmine leaned in with a knowing smile.

"You did great. And remember—we're all in this together."

Haylee smiled back, something inside her settling.

"Thanks, Jasmine. For everything."

Because sometimes, the most powerful mentors are the ones who simply walk beside you—no spotlight, no script. Just the truth.
And a shared road.

Chapter 8:
Setbacks and Second-Guessing

By week three, Haylee was ready to set Bertha on fire and disappear into the woods.

She stood barefoot on the RV's half-tiled floor, palms sticky with failed adhesive, surrounded by piles of "what the hell was I thinking?" and half-finished chaos. The washer-dryer combo had shorted the inverter. The solar setup wouldn't hold a charge. And her Pinterest-perfect backsplash dream had devolved into a crooked mess of warped peel-and-stick tiles and smeared grout.

Bertha looked like a dorm room had exploded inside a garage sale.
Haylee slumped into the reading nook, every muscle in her back screaming. Her phone buzzed. A message from her old college roommate lit up the screen:
"You okay? Maybe it's time to come back to reality? You don't have to prove anything to anyone."
A second pinged in:
"So when are you gonna stop playing HGTV and get back to real life?"

Haylee stared at the texts like they were written in a language she used to speak but no longer understood. Once, those people had been her lifeline. Now they felt like static.
What exactly was "real life," anyway?
Working herself into burnout? Pretending she didn't notice Jake's growing indifference? Filing expense reports and replying to emails until her soul evaporated?

She stood and paced Bertha's length, fists clenched. Maybe this whole thing was ridiculous. Maybe she was having a breakdown. Maybe everyone was right.

She grabbed Aggie's journal, ready to slam it shut for good, when something fluttered loose from the back. A folded note, tucked into the spine. Not part of the binding. Just waiting.

"Haylee—
You'll have days when everything breaks.
When the tiles don't stick and the genny won't run and the people you thought you could count on forget how to show up.
That's when you keep going.
Because if you only build on the easy days, you'll never finish a thing worth standing in."

She read it again. And again. Then taped the note above the sink and stood in the middle of the mess like a woman who'd just remembered her name.
She picked up the tools.
Re-leveled the backsplash.
Ripped out the faulty wiring and called Benny.
Rewatched Aggie fixing the generator until she got it right.

Then she drove an hour out of town and bought a secondhand lithium battery setup off a guy from Craigslist—miracle of miracles, it actually worked.
That night, back at the park, a neighbor two spots down lit a grill and waved her over.
"You're the one with the mystery RV, right?" the woman asked, laughing. "Saw you out here muttering at a generator like it owed you money."

"Guilty," Haylee said, smiling despite herself.

She stayed for a drink. Left smelling like woodsmoke, armed with half a dozen road-life hacks and a quiet but powerful reminder:
She wasn't alone. Not out here. Not in this.

Bertha's Second Life

Haylee stood barefoot on Bertha's original flooring—old hardwood but good bones. In one hand, a soft green paint swatch labeled Wanderlust. In the other, a screwdriver. The cabinet door had just fallen off again.
She sighed. "Okay, old girl. Let's see what you're hiding."

Kneeling down, she set the swatch on the counter and worked the last remaining hinge loose. The cabinet creaked as she pulled it open fully, revealing a tangle of mouse-chewed insulation and what looked suspiciously like a hand-scrawled recipe card wedged behind a broken shelf bracket.

Bertha, as Aggie had affectionately named the Class C motorhome, was as stubborn as she was charming. Every inch creaked with history. Every layer of wallpaper whispered a decade's worth of decisions. And Haylee, three weeks into her full-time renovation gamble, was finally beginning to learn that restoring an RV was less about control and more about conversation.

She tilted her head, holding the card up to the light. The ink was faded but legible: Aggie's Pickled Okra – Do not substitute! Trust me. Haylee chuckled.

"That you, Aggie? You trying to feed me from beyond the grave?"

The wind rustled through the cracked kitchen window, as if answering. Haylee felt a familiar flutter of goosebumps across her arms. She rubbed them absentmindedly and turned her attention back to the cabinet. A small, square opening in the back panel caught her eye—something she hadn't noticed before.

Prying gently with the screwdriver, she popped the panel loose. Inside was a bundle wrapped in oilcloth, dry and stiff with age. Carefully unrolling it, she discovered a handful of yellowed photographs, a rusted skeleton key, and a folded letter addressed simply: Haylee-girl.

Haylee sat back on her heels, heart beating a little faster now. The letter crackled as she unfolded it, its corners fragile with time. The handwriting was slanted and elegant, ink slightly smudged in places as if written in a hurry—or with emotion.

If you've found this, then Bertha has chosen you. Don't laugh. She doesn't open up for just anyone. I saw Bertha not as she was, but as she could be. And she rewarded me in ways that defied logic and time.

Haylee paused, goosebumps rising again—not from the cold this time.

There are parts of this RV that don't show themselves until you're ready. Things that weren't here yesterday. Secrets that don't appear unless you need them. I know how that sounds. But I promise, if you listen—really listen—Bertha will show you everything. Just don't rush her.

The letter ended with a strange set of symbols: a circle around a key, and what looked like three vertical lines radiating outward like rays. Below it, a simple postscript: P.S. Bertha is more than she seems.

Haylee sat still for a long moment, the walls humming around her. Outside, a car passed on the street. Inside, the silence was thicker than before—as if Bertha herself were holding her breath, waiting to see what she'd do next.

She tucked the letter back into the oilcloth and held the key in her palm, its teeth cold and sharp. She stood slowly, eyes drifting upward toward the ceiling. The soft green paint swatch fluttered to the floor, forgotten.

"Okay," she whispered. "Keep your secrets ol' girl, for now."

Haylee lifted the bed to the storage underneath. A dust-scented air that carried the faintest trace of lilac.

That scent again. She'd caught it before, always faint and fleeting—never strong enough to trace. But now it poured from beneath the bed like a memory too strong to hide.

She wedged a piece of wood under the lid to hold it up, "I'll have to put in struts later" she thought to herself.

Haylee climbed in, the key still in her pocket. The storage was dim but not dark. Sunlight filtered through the top. Dust swirled in the beam like tiny stars in a galaxy long forgotten.

Then she saw it.

A trunk sat in the center of the floor, perfectly clean, untouched by dust. Its brass fittings shimmered softly, as though just polished. Around it, the air seemed denser. Charg ed.

Haylee leaned forward, heart knocking like a warning. She pulled the trunk closer to her. There was a key hole similar to the key in her pocket. She slipped the key into the lock. It turned easily. Too easily.

The trunk could barely open under the bed. So Haylee pulled it completely out and set it on the floor in the kitchen.

Inside lay a velvet-lined interior, deep purple and improbably pristine. A bundle of dried flowers rested atop an old journal wrapped in silk ribbon. Beneath that, more photographs—Aggie standing in front of Bertha, decade after decade, smiling with the same quiet confidence she always had. Haylee realized. Just like the letter said.

But then—movement.

In the far corner of the RV, the shadows shifted. Not like something had moved. More like the shadows themselves *were* moving. A figure began to form—not fully solid, not entirely there—a soft outline of a woman in a long dress, her face indistinct but kind.

Haylee's breath caught.
The figure raised a hand slowly and pointed—not at Haylee, but at the trunk beside her.
Haylee turned.

There, in the corner of the trunk, a strange symbol had begun to glow—the same one from the letter: a circle around a key, three lines radiating outward. The lining looked... loose. Like a secret hidden in plain sight.

She turned back, but the figure was gone. Only the scent of lilac remained.

Heart pounding, Haylee reached for the lining; being careful not to destroy anything.

She reached in, fingers brushing the faintly glowing symbol. The warmth pulsed once beneath her touch—gentle, like a heartbeat. But just as she pressed in, the glow dimmed. The symbol faded.

Whatever it was… it wasn't ready. Or maybe she wasn't.

Haylee exhaled, a slow breath she hadn't realized she was holding. "Okay. Not today."

The journal called to her. She picked it up, feeling its weight, the silk ribbon barely holding the weathered pages together. Inside, a name was scrawled in the front: Agnes Hensen – Spring, 1972.

She stood and returned the trunk under the bed.

She turned a few pages, eyes scanning faded ink and looping script. Notes about renovations, sketches of possible layouts, but also entries about dreams—vivid, strange ones. Mentions of voices. Shifting items. The way the RV seemed to respond.

One entry stopped her cold.

Bertha opens herself slowly. "It's not just the interior that changes." "It's you." "I've started hearing footsteps at night. Not mine. And the lilacs. Always lilacs, when something's coming."

Haylee closed the journal slowly and set it back in the trunk. She would read more —but later. Bit by bit. Just like Bertha wanted.

As she left the bedroom, she noticed the scent of lilac was gone. The RV felt calm. Watching, maybe. Waiting.

Back in the kitchen, the sunlight had shifted, golden and soft. The paint swatch lay where it had fallen—Wanderlust.

She picked it up and smiled. "All right, old girl. Let's start with the walls. You keep your secrets… for now." And Bertha, silent and stoic, seemed to agree.

Supplies & Support

Fixing Bertha was equal parts thrilling and exhausting. So she started small:

- Created a checklist: Electrical, Plumbing, Interior, Comfort.
- Ordered tile for the floors, cabinet handles, and weather tape from a big-box store.
- Ordered struts to hold the bed up; to access the storage underneath.
- Hired Denny, a mobile RV tech with a beard longer than her grocery list, to inspect the propane system.
- Buck showed her how to swap out a faulty converter.
-

Jasmine loaned her a paint sprayer—which she immediately clogged for not thinning the paint.

Bertha became a construction zone.
By weeks end, she had:

■ Replaced the dinette with a cozy reading nook filled with floor cushions and string lights

■ Installed a washer-dryer combo (three hours of swearing, one YouTube tutorial)

■ Swapped yellowed blinds for soft linen curtains

■ Mounted a spice rack and glued a tiny crystal from Aggie to the corner like a quiet talisman

Memory Lane & Emotional Depth

One afternoon, while cleaning an overhead bin, Haylee found a stack of old postcards. Addressed to her—from Aggie.

Her hands trembled as she read:

"Sedona this week. The rocks are red and stubborn—just like you were at ten. :)"

"Met a woman with two dogs and one leg. She laughed more than anyone I've ever met."

"Life is weird and good and beautiful. Please don't forget that."

Haylee cried harder than she expected—not from guilt, but from longing. She missed that curious, unguarded girl her aunt had believed in so fiercely.

RV Park Shenanigans

Meanwhile, the park remained its usual delightful chaos:
Lenny set off his smoke alarm making "van lasagna."

Marlene's psychic cat kept sleeping on Haylee's solar panel box. ("She says it'll work better now.")

Lou offered to help install the inverter, then tripped on Disco the goat and broke her drill.

Jake (yes, that Jake) left a voicemail she didn't return. And didn't feel tempted to.

Instead, she kept sanding. Painting. Measuring.
Bertha wasn't just a vehicle now. She was a promise.
One evening, after a particularly satisfying round of flooring, Haylee sat outside with a cup of tea. Bertha looked different—still old, still dented, but unmistakably hers.
Mavis plopped into the next chair. "You've really made her shine. Aggie would've loved to have seen what you've done."
"I hope so," Haylee whispered.
"You ready for your first trip soon?"
She looked at the travel guides stacked nearby. Aggie's journal was open in her lap, bookmarked with a pressed flower.
"Almost," she said. "Just a few more things to finish. Then... the road."
Bertha smelled faintly of lemon and sage from the homemade cleaner. The new floors clicked softly under her boots. The thrifted curtains swayed gently in the breeze.
Every detail whispered: *home.*

The Solar Whisperer

One problem remained: Bertha had no off-grid power.

Hookups were fine. But boondocking—camping off-grid—meant full self-reliance. No plug-ins. No safety net.

She added the newest (and most daunting) item to her to-do list:

- Solar Panels + Inverter for Lithium Setup

Two days later, a dusty van pulled into the lot. A ladder strapped on top. A man stepped out.

"Is this the solar job for the vintage Class C with the pastel flower stickers?" he asked.

"That's the one," Haylee said, gesturing to Bertha.

Leo was younger than expected—mid-twenties, sun-streaked hair, toolbox in each hand, and the kind of calm that suggested he'd never rushed a day in his life. He came highly recommended by three RVers in the park.

"She's a little temperamental," Haylee warned as he climbed up to inspect the roof. "She's a legend," he said, running a hand over the paneling. "I've worked on school buses, horse trailers, even a hearse. But none with this much personality."

Over two days, Leo installed:
A 400W solar array

A Victron inverter

A charge controller

Two 100Ah lithium batteries, tucked into a modified cabinet

Haylee hovered with a notebook, scribbling notes she barely understood. Leo was patient, explaining wattage, charge curves, and inverter types. She nodded like she understood on the second try.

A Setback—and a Lesson

On day two, Haylee offered to connect the batteries.
"I watched three tutorials," she said confidently.
Fifteen minutes later, she blew a fuse.
"Okay, I watched parts of three tutorials," she admitted.

Leo laughed, unfazed. "You'd be shocked how many people short their system with a coffee maker. You're doing great."

When he finished, the panels gleamed like small, silent promises. Haylee flipped the switch on the charge controller—and the lights came on.
She gasped. Then clapped her hands. "It worked!"

Leo tipped an invisible hat. "Welcome to power freedom."

Reflective Moment

That night, Haylee lay under her fairy lights. The laptop charged quietly beside her. The fridge hummed—on solar.

And for the first time, she felt it in her bones:
She didn't need Jake.
She didn't need a three-bedroom house.
She didn't need permission.
She had light. She had a home.
She had herself.

She looked out the window at the moon above the treetops. Aggie had chased stars across state lines.
Now Haylee could, too.
And this time, she didn't have to wait for anyone.

Chapter 9:
Blank Pages and New Words

The next morning, Haylee woke before sunrise.

No alarm. No blinking email notifications. No frantic to-do list buzzing in her brain.

Just birdsong. And the soft, rhythmic creak of Bertha settling in the cool morning air.

She wrapped herself in a blanket, made coffee on the tiny propane stove—successfully this time—and sat in the nook she'd built with her own hands. The stick-on flooring still buckled slightly near the bathroom, and the backsplash had a corner that refused to sit flat, but Bertha was starting to feel less like a project and more like home.

She opened Aggie's notebook and flipped past the blank pages to the one with the note.

Then, she turned to a clean sheet.

And Haylee started to write.

Not to be productive. Not to submit. Not to "build her brand."

Just to breathe.

At first, it was simple:

Day 26. Bertha smells like dust and coffee and cedarwood cleaner. I think I'm finally okay with that.

Learned how to reset the solar inverter today. Also learned I'm stronger than I give myself credit for.

Talked to a woman from Montana who lives with two dogs and a cat in an Airstream. She says freedom tastes like cold beer and fireflies.

I believe her, as Aunt Aggie would say.

She didn't stop. The words spilled out like they'd been waiting—like the silence of her old life had been starving them.

She wrote until the coffee went cold and her hand cramped. Then she opened her laptop and published her first video on YouTube.

"Burnout, Backlash, and Bertha: How Losing Everything Made Me Start Living"

No filter. No branding. Just honesty.

She added a few raw photos—renovation chaos, her sitting barefoot on Bertha's step with a mug, the old VHS tape and camcorder tape beside her aunt's journal.

She hit publish before she could talk herself out of it.

An hour later, there were two comments. Then five. Then twelve.

One was from a woman named Jess:

"I didn't even know I was holding my breath until I read this."

Another read:

"I quit my job last month and thought I was insane. Now I think maybe I'm brave."

Haylee sat back and stared at the screen.

People were listening.

Not the way they had when she was a bookkeeper—where everything was data and invoices and polite protocol—but truly listening.

The kind that happens when someone sees you.

When your truth resonates like a tuning fork in someone else's chest.

She wasn't just surviving anymore.

She was telling her story.

And it mattered.

She didn't know what the future looked like. She still didn't have a five-year plan.

But for the first time in her adult life, she wasn't just reacting to the world.

Test Run and Tails

It was finally happening.

Bertha was stocked, solar-equipped, and freshly swept.

Haylee had filled her pantry with shelf-stable meals, coffee, and an arguably excessive amount of peanut butter and dog food. There were folded road maps in the glovebox and a cooler of produce from the local farmers market.

And now, she had a co-pilot.

A two-year-old mutt from the shelter—part lab, part shepherd, and part joyful chaos. Haylee had gone "just to look" the week before, but the moment she locked eyes with the scruffy, tawny dog curled in the back kennel, she knew she wasn't leaving alone.

She named her Josie, after her aunt's middle name—Josephine.

"She's shy at first," the shelter staff had warned. "But she's a total shadow once she trusts you."

Now, Josie sat perched on the passenger seat like she was born to ride shotgun, ears perked, tail thumping with cautious excitement.

Haylee typed the destination into the GPS:

Cedar Willow State Park.

Just two hours from the RV park, it was the perfect beginner's escape—quiet, scenic, with hiking trails, a creek, and no hookups. A dry site. A true test for the solar setup.

Getting there… wasn't exactly smooth.

She took a wrong turn, forgot to latch a cabinet (sending cereal flying), and stalled Bertha twice at stop signs.

But when they finally rolled into site #13—tucked between pines, overlooking a still lake—Haylee felt breathless in the best way.

She had done it.

The First Night

Josie sniffed every pine needle and rock while Haylee set up camp. She unrolled her folding chair, laid out a small mat at the door, and poured wine into a metal camp cup.

Birdsong filled the evening air. No traffic. No notifications.

No Jake.

As dusk settled, she cooked a simple dinner on the camp stove—veggie tacos and roasted corn—then curled up outside, Josie snuggled at her feet.

That's when she remembered the postcards.

She opened Aggie's journal to the page with the pressed wildflower and tucked note:

"If you ever feel unsure—go to Cedar Willow. There's a tree there I carved my name into when I was 19. Under the lookout bluff. Give her my love."

Haylee blinked.

Aggie had been here. Walked these same trails. Maybe sat at this very site, barefoot and laughing with strangers.

The next morning, Haylee packed a daypack, leashed up Josie, and set off for the bluff.

The Carved Tree

The hike took nearly an hour. Josie trotted ahead, then circled back often to nudge Haylee's leg like a fuzzy, four-legged life coach.

At the summit, the lake stretched below like glass, rimmed by forest and morning sky.

And there it was.

An old oak tree, bark thick and gnarled, initials carved into its base:

AH – '85

And just beneath it, faint but legible:

"This life is mine."

Haylee knelt and traced the letters with her fingers. Then sat beneath the tree, Josie leaning into her side.

Tears welled up—not from grief, but from recognition.

This was the beginning. Aggie had carved it in her way.

Now, Haylee was carving hers. She carved her initials under her aunt's carving.

HH - '24, "Here is where mine begins."

Camping Quirks and Quiet Joys

That night, Haylee:
– Used the wrong inverter setting and accidentally turned off her fridge
(miraculously, nothing spoiled).
– Woke at 3 a.m. convinced a raccoon was staging a break-in.
– Watched Josie chase a moth in her sleep and snore like a cartoon grandfather.
– Made coffee on the camp stove and watched the sunrise through Bertha's
window, tears warm in her eyes.

She was still learning. Still fumbling.
But she was living.

Chapter 10:
An Invitation, a Map, and a Choice

It started with a knock.
Haylee opened Bertha's door to find Marla standing there with a creased manila envelope tucked under one arm and a coffee thermos in the other.

"Found this in Aggie's storage box," Marla said. "Figured it was time."

Inside the envelope: a folded paper map of the American Southwest, worn soft at the edges and covered in highlighter swirls and Aggie's looping handwriting. There were tiny hearts in the margins. Circles around offbeat towns. Hiking trails marked with phrases like "healing creek" and "sky full of stars—stay two nights!" In the top right corner, written in red ink:
"For Haylee, if she ever finds her fire again."

Haylee's throat tightened. "She really thought of everything, didn't she?"
Marla nodded. "Aggie wasn't just trying to leave you an RV," she said. "She was trying to leave you a life. The kind she knew you'd forgotten how to want."

They sat outside in folding chairs, sipping coffee while the map flapped lazily between them. Marla pointed to a heart drawn near a small town in New Mexico. "Taos. We used to go every October. Aggie always said, 'If you ever came back to yourself, that's where you should begin.'"

Haylee stared at the constellation of places Aggie had marked—scattered stars on faded paper—and could already feel the road calling.
Bertha humming beneath her. Her notebook opened in the passenger seat. Miles of story waiting to be written.

"Is that why she prepaid the RV spot for a month?" Haylee asked, a small smile for ming.
Marla grinned. "She figured you'd need just long enough to talk yourself into it."

Back inside, Haylee pulled out her laptop and opened YouTube. She uploaded a new video:
"My Aunt Left Me a Map, and I Think I'm Going to Follow It."

The response was immediate. Comments flooded in: someone recommended their favorite campground in Arizona; someone else linked to a freelance writing job board. A third shared photos of their own renovated campervan.

She wasn't talking into the void anymore. She was reaching a community that had been waiting—people who only needed one person to say "me too" first.

By sunset, Haylee had made a list:

- Install backup water pump
- Fix that creaky cabinet door
- Apply for at least two remote writing gigs
- Map a rough route to Taos
-
- And at the bottom, scribbled in her own looping scrawl:
- ***Don't chicken out. Not this time.***
-

That night, she fell asleep to the soft rhythm of rain tapping on Bertha's roof. Not a storm. Just a gentle, steady applause—like the world quietly celebrating her first brave yes.

She dreamt of desert skies. Of canyon echoes. Of Aggie by a fire, grinning.

"About damn time."

Uninvited Guests, Unexpected Gifts

Haylee wasn't expecting company when she returned to Bertha after a morning hike with Josie. The trail had stretched longer than planned—Josie, ever the curious pup, had stopped at every fern, every fallen pinecone, sniffing them like each one held an ancient secret. By the time they reached Site #13, Haylee's stomach growled louder than the creek below.

But as they approached Bertha's driver's side, something unusual caught her eye. A tail.

Long. Gray. Flicking lazily in the sunlight, which was filtering through the windshield like a soft spotlight.

Josie froze at her side, ears alert, but calm. No growl, no stiffened stance—just a curious tilt of her head. She seemed... unbothered.

Haylee squinted.

Curled in the driver's seat, like she had every right to be there, was a sleek little cat —her fur a beautiful mix of mottled silver and smoky gray, the kind that made her look like she'd been painted in soft shades of twilight. She had enormous green eyes, wide and curious, and a dainty pink nose that twitched as it sniffed the air. The cat blinked at her slowly, the kind of deliberate gaze that only cats can give—a look of assessment, then comfort, as if she was deciding whether to stay or leave. Then she tucked her paws beneath her chest and let out a soft, almost imperceptible purr, her body still curled into a perfect little ball of serenity.

"Well," Haylee murmured, more to herself than anything, "you've really made yourself at home."

She slowly set her water bottle down, not wanting to startle the cat. The air between them felt... charged, like there was an understanding that had passed unspoken. Something about the cat's calm presence seemed to suggest that she'd been here longer than the few hours since Haylee had left for her hike.

"Josie, what do you think?" Haylee whispered, her eyes flicking from the cat to her dog. Josie's tail wagged lazily, but the dog didn't bark or lunge. She stood quietly beside Haylee, waiting for the next move.

Haylee was hesitant at first, unsure if the cat was just a lost wanderer or if she had adopted Bertha as her new home. She walked slowly toward the side of the RV, careful not to make any sudden movements. She didn't want to startle the little creature but also didn't know what else to do.

The cat, noticing the approach, tilted her head to the side. She was not afraid. Not even wary. Just... watching. After a few seconds, she stretched one sleek paw and then slowly extended her back, arching her body in a feline yawn.

"All right then," Haylee said softly, bending down to scoop up a small piece of salmon jerky from her bag. It wasn't much, but it might be enough to coax her.

The cat's nose twitched at the scent of the jerky. She didn't rush, but after a few beats, she slid out of the driver's seat with graceful slowness. She padded to Haylee, her paws silent on the gravel, and sniffed the treat.

Haylee held her breath as the cat sniffed the air, then reached out a paw to gently touch the jerky. When she nibbled at it, Haylee's heart gave a quiet flutter. The cat wasn't feral; she wasn't starving. She was just... a cat with a quiet confidence.

"There you go," Haylee whispered. She scratched behind the cat's ears. The purring that followed was soft and immediate, the vibration filling the space between them, grounding the moment in something simple, yet deeply reassuring.

No collar. No tag. No sign of ownership.

Haylee was about to ask around when the thought crossed her mind—what if she's not lost?

She posted a notice at the ranger station, asking anyone in the park if they recognized the little creature. No one did.

"She's probably a trail cat," Buck had told her later over the phone. "Sometimes they're born out here. Campers feed 'em, and they stick around. But if she picked you? That's something. She don't just go with anyone."

A Name and a Bond

That night, as Haylee sat outside, writing in her journal under the vast sky, the cat curled up in her lap. Josie lay at her feet, her gentle snores mingling with the quiet murmur of the wind. It was the first time in what felt like forever that Haylee had truly felt at peace—no deadlines, no noise, no expectations—just this little patch of earth, this tiny family she had found in the most unexpected way.

Haylee's fingers hovered over the pages of her journal, the soft purring of Belle—a name that came to her like an echo of something older, softer—reminding her of how much had changed in such a short time.

"You're beautiful," she murmured to the cat, whose green eyes blinked lazily up at her. "Belle."

The cat's eyes flicked open. A small glimmer of acknowledgment, or perhaps it was simply a cat's natural curiosity. She stretched and curled tighter in her lap, a slight purr of contentment rumbling against her chest.

Haylee smiled softly, a thought striking her in the quiet space.

"No," she said aloud to herself, "Bella. For the beauty. And because everything feels a little softer with an 'a.'"

She gently ran her fingers through the cat's fur, feeling the weight of the moment settle over her like the twilight sky.

Bella wasn't just a stray. She wasn't a random interruption. She was part of this. A companion for the road ahead. A reminder of the unexpected gifts the world offered if you were open enough to receive them.

The Spark of a Dream

That name, Bella, lingered with Haylee even after they left Cedar Willow two days later. Bertha rumbled along the backroads, the gentle hum of the engine mingling with the sound of Josie's panting from the open window and Bella's soft purring from her perch on the dashboard. The name Bella stuck with her. The cat. The beauty. *French.* Her aunt had once said, "You should learn it. It's the language of poets and people who drink coffee slowly." Haylee had never made the time, and had never thought she could. There was always something else—work, deadlines, obligations. But now? She reached for her phone, pulled up an app, and downloaded it.

French, Beginner. Daily Practice: 10 minutes.
She said the first word aloud to no one but herself.

"Bonjour."

Bella blinked from her perch. Josie barked in response. Haylee laughed. It was the kind of laughter that came from deep within, a release of months, maybe years, of tension she hadn't even known she was holding.
The road stretched ahead. Bella, Josie, and the world were all hers for the taking. And for the first time, Haylee felt like she was truly free to follow wherever the journey led.

Chapter 11:
Leaving, and Saying Goodbye

The morning Haylee packed up Bertha was quiet. The RV park was still half asleep, with only a couple of the long-term campers out on their early morning walks. Haylee folded clothes, tucked away loose items, and arranged everything with purpose, even though she still didn't fully know where the journey was headed. But she knew she was going. Finally.
The road was calling.

As she stashed away the last of the kitchen supplies, she heard the unmistakable hum of a familiar engine firing to life. Haylee turned and saw Jake's car pull into the parking lot. He had been trying to reach her for days—sending texts, leaving voicemails, all of which she hadn't bothered to return.
This was it. The last meeting.

Her stomach twisted, but her resolve stayed firm. She had made her choice. And this was just one last piece of her old life to move out of the way.

She stepped out of Bertha, shielding her eyes from the early sun, and watched as Jake climbed out of his car, hands stuffed in his hoodie pockets. He looked the same—same relaxed slouch, same half-smile that used to make her heart skip. Josie sat up in the passenger seat, alert, watching Haylee for any sign of unease. Bella, however, looked up briefly from her perch on the dashboard but quickly laid back down, uninterested.

"Hay... I mean Haylee," he called, his voice tentative, like he wasn't sure whether he still had the right to use her name. "Can we talk?"

She nodded, crossing her arms and leaning against the side of Bertha. "I figured this was coming. What's on your mind, Jake?"

He hesitated, biting his lip before taking a deep breath and stepping closer, avoiding her gaze. "I know I wasn't exactly what you needed. And I get why you left. But... I don't know, Hay. We were together for ten years. That means something."

Haylee didn't answer right away. Instead, she ran her fingers along the edge of Bertha's doorframe, the cool metal grounding her. This place—this thing—was her choice now. Not his.

"Ten years," she repeated softly, almost to herself. "Yeah, it did mean something. But it doesn't mean we were right for each other. Not anymore."

Jake's jaw tightened, frustration creeping into his features. "So this is it? You're just… going to leave?" His voice was rising now, tinged with anger. "You think just walking away is going to fix everything? You think you can just drop everything, Haylee, and start over like nothing happened?"

The words were laced with guilt—his usual tactic. He wasn't going to let her leave without making her feel like it was her fault.

Haylee swallowed hard, her heart squeezing a little, but she stood her ground. "Yeah, I am. I'm not running away, Jake. I'm starting over. Something I should have done a long time ago."

He scoffed, shaking his head in disbelief. "You can't seriously be this cold. After everything we've been through? You're just going to throw it all away? What, because now you found some new life? Some adventure? What about us, Haylee? What about me?"

His words were sharp, hitting that familiar note of self-centeredness, as if he believed he was the one who had been wronged. It wasn't a surprise—he always had a way of making her feel like the bad guy, even when he was the one who hadn't changed.

Her chest tightened, but she pushed past it. "You don't get it. This isn't about you. This is about me finally living my life the way I need to. Not because of you, or for you, but for me. We're not meant to be together anymore."

Jake took a deep breath, his hands fidgeting in his pockets as he stared at the ground. Then he looked up at her, the pain in his eyes softening into something almost like regret.

"You're really serious about this," he said quietly, almost like he couldn't believe it.

"I am," she replied, her voice steady. "It's time."

A heavy silence settled between them. Jake ran a hand through his messy hair, his frustration shifting into something that bordered on self-pity. "I never thought it would end like this. I guess I always thought I'd get another chance to… change. But you were right. I didn't try. I stayed stuck. And you—you're out there doing things. Living. While I… I'm just sitting here, waiting for things to get better. Waiting for you to come back."

His words stung, not because they were true, but because he still thought she was the one who could fix everything. As if her leaving was just another step in his own timeline of waiting for the right moment to change. He was still making it about him.

She could feel her chest tighten again, but she pressed on. "Jake, this isn't about waiting. You've had plenty of time. I've given you plenty of time. But you were too busy holding onto what was comfortable instead of working for something better. I don't owe you another chance."

He sighed, his shoulders slumping as though defeated. "I'm sorry, Haylee. I'm sorry for not seeing you, for not seeing what you needed. I… I hope you find whatever it is you're looking for. I really do. But, damn, I thought we were worth fighting for. I thought you'd fight for me, for us."

For a moment, Haylee thought she might cry. She thought of everything they'd been—good and bad—and realized just how much of herself she'd lost in trying to make it work. But the tears didn't come. Instead, she felt a quiet peace settle in her chest.

"I'm sorry too," she said, her voice clear and unhurried. "I didn't make it easy. But I need to do this for me now. Not for you. Not for anyone."

Jake nodded, but his expression was distant. He looked like he wanted to say more, but it wasn't the right moment.

He shifted uncomfortably on his feet, and after a long, drawn-out silence, he finally said, "Well, I guess this is goodbye then?"

Haylee felt the weight of finality in his words. This was it. No more second chances. No more excuses. Just two people who had shared a chapter, and now had to turn the page.

"Yeah," she whispered, her voice steady. "Goodbye."

Jake hesitated for a moment, then stepped forward, pulling her into a brief, awkward hug. It wasn't the kind of hug that spoke of longing or reconciliation. It was a goodbye, plain and simple—a gesture to close the door without slamming it.

When he pulled away, he gave her one last, uncertain smile. "Take care of yourself, Haylee."
"You too, Jake."

He climbed back into his car and drove away, his engine fading into the distance. Haylee stood there for a long moment, watching the dust settle behind him. It wasn't dramatic, and it wasn't full of bitter words. It was just… done. Josie lay at Haylee's feet, content and calm in her presence.

She closed the door to Bertha and stood there for a long time, her back pressed against the cool metal. She let the weight of it all sink in. This was her life now.

She reached down, giving Josie a gentle pet, then ushered her to the passenger seat, where Bella had already made herself comfortable on the dash, soaking in the warm sunlight.

She wasn't going back to the life she'd left behind. She wasn't going to pretend anymore that the old world could work for her. She had changed. The life ahead would be messy, hard, and completely unknown—but it was hers.

With a deep breath, Haylee climbed into the driver seat, started the engine, and with a smile at Josie and Bella, pulled out of the RV park.
The open road was waiting.

Chapter 12:
The Road Begins

The road stretched out ahead, flat and golden under the early sun, a ribbon of freedom unfurling one mile at a time. Haylee couldn't remember the last time she had felt this awake—truly awake. Something in the way the horizon reached endlessly forward made her lungs feel bigger, like she could finally breathe without bracing.

Bertha hummed beneath her hands, steady and familiar, the rhythm of her engine syncing with Haylee's heartbeat. The dashboard bobbed gently with the bumps in the pavement, and her girls—Josie sprawled on the passenger seat, Bella a quiet sentinel on the dash—dozed peacefully as the landscape slid by.

She had no exact destination. And for once, that wasn't scary.
It was liberating.

Her phone buzzed in the cup holder. A voicemail from her dad.
"Hope you're doing okay. I'm proud of you, kid. Just make sure you don't forget to check in now and then. Love you."

A small smile tugged at her lips. It wasn't dramatic or poetic—but it was real. Her dad had always struggled with emotions, always more comfortable fixing things than saying how he felt. But still, here he was—trying. That meant something.

A few hours later, Haylee pulled into a gravel lot next to a faded diner between two gas stations. The sign out front, missing a few bulbs, read **"Homemade Pie & Honest Coffee"** in flaking red paint.

She walked Josie first, then cracked a window for Bella, who blinked at her lazily from her sunbeam throne.
Inside, the diner smelled like bacon grease and syrup, and a Patsy Cline song played low and ghostly on a jukebox in the corner. Haylee slid into a booth by the window, heart full and a little hollow at the same time.

A waitress with a tight bun and kind, weathered eyes handed her a menu.

"You traveling?" she asked, as if she already knew.

Haylee nodded. "Just starting out."

The woman smiled, approving. "Good. Life's too short to sit still and wonder."

Haylee smiled back, the simple exchange filling something in her chest she hadn't known was empty.

She ordered coffee and pie—apple, thick with cinnamon and a little too sweet, but exactly what she needed. Josie's nose poked up through the cracked window, tail wagging at the scent. Bella had vanished to the back of Bertha, but Haylee knew she'd emerge at exactly the right time—as she always did.

While she ate, she opened her journal and wrote:

The road isn't just a place to go. It's a place to become. To remember who I was when the world still felt wide open.

She lingered for a while, the diner's quiet becoming a kind of balm. When she paid, the waitress handed back her receipt with a knowing smile.

"Take pictures," she said. "Of everything. Even the quiet moments—especially those."

Haylee nodded, unexpectedly choked up. "I will."

Back at Bertha, she handed Josie a bite of leftover crust. The dog took it with gentle enthusiasm and hopped into the passenger seat. Bella, ever elegant, emerged from the back, stretching like she'd just returned from her own internal journey. Haylee looked at them both—her found family—and realized they each carried a story. Each had been lost, or abandoned, or just unsure.

But now?

Now, they were heading somewhere—together.

The road opened up again, sun hanging high above the desert hills, and Haylee drove with one hand on the wheel and the other resting lightly on the journal in her lap. There was still fear in her chest, still that lingering question: Am I doing the right thing? But mile by mile, the fear was softening. It wasn't running anymore. It was becoming. Reclaiming.

She wasn't the same woman who had shown up to Cedar Willow with a packed bag and shaking hands.

By late afternoon, the sun dipped low enough to tint everything in warm amber. She pulled into a rustic campground just outside a town too small for cell signal but big enough to have a name painted on an old water tower.

She set up camp, walked Josie beneath the cottonwoods, then lit a small fire as dusk settled in. Bella nestled in her lap. Josie stretched beside her, ears twitching in a dream.

Coyotes howled somewhere in the distance, and above them, the stars blinked into place—like tiny promises she hadn't yet unwrapped.

This was only the beginning.

Dust, Dreams, and the Open Road

She hadn't planned on finding the festival.

Haylee was only supposed to stop in the small desert town of Sable Rock for the night—refill water, pick up local honey, and keep rolling. But as Bertha crested the hill into town, she slowed on instinct.

Because spread across the dry basin like a strange, joyful mirage was a pop-up village of color and music and motion.

A painted sign at the entrance read:

✨ MIRAGE FESTIVAL – CREATIVITY UNLEASHED ✨
 Live music. Art. Workshops. Kind humans welcome.

Bertha rolled forward like she already knew.

Sable Rock's festival wasn't huge, but it was alive.

There were hand woven tapestries dancing in the wind. Crystals lined up on burlap tables. Solar-powered art stations. A woman read tarot near a bus painted in moon phases. Children chalked mandalas onto the pavement. A musician strummed a banjo made from an old oil can.

Haylee parked on the edge of it all. Josie at her side. Bella followed silently, curious but graceful, like a ghost slipping through a crowd.

She wandered the festival, bartered a spare flashlight for a hand-stitched journal from a woman named Sol.

"Every traveler needs somewhere to write it down," Sol said, adjusting her enormous straw hat.

"I think I do," Haylee replied, cradling the book.

Later, while sipping hibiscus lemonade by the fire circle, she met Isaac—a sculptor who lived in a vintage ambulance-turned-studio.

They talked about grief and clay and people who never left their hometowns. He reminded her of someone Aggie would've liked.

"My brother thinks I've lost it," he said, "but I've never felt more grounded."

"Same," she smiled. "Turns out being a little 'lost' is exactly how I found this."

He grinned. "Then you're in the right place."

On the last night of the festival, an open mic was held under a solar-lit dome. Someone wheeled in an upright piano. A teenager played a haunting melody on a musical saw.

Haylee was nervous, but she stepped up. Her girls flanked her—Josie by the stage, Bella weaving between ankles like a shadow.

She opened her journal and read:

"I used to live in a world that paid me for hours, not for heart.
I used to be afraid of silence.
I used to mistake stillness for stagnation.
But now?
I wake to the sound of my own breath and the sunrise.
I move not to arrive, but to become."

The crowd clapped, soft and sincere.
And Haylee?
She didn't cry.
She glowed.

The applause faded gently, like ripples on water, and Haylee stepped down from the stage feeling dazed—not from nerves, but from something else. Something quieter, deeper. A kind of release.

She had told the truth, aloud, to strangers. And instead of silence or polite disinterest, they had offered her warmth. Not just with their clapping, but with their faces—soft, open, affirming. It wasn't fame. It wasn't validation in the old way. It was recognition. She felt seen—not for who she'd been expected to be, but for who she truly was becoming.

Isaac met her at the bottom of the steps with two tin mugs of warm cider and a crooked grin. "That was beautiful," he said. "Raw. Real. You write like someone who's stopped pretending."

Haylee accepted the cider and laughed, more grateful than she could say. "I think I've spent most of my life trying to earn the wrong kind of approval."

"Well," he shrugged, "sounds like you just stopped asking permission."

They walked back toward the fire circle, where a woman with a harmonium had started singing in a soft, undulating tone. Someone else joined in on hand drums.

The mood had shifted—less performative now, more communal. People curled into blankets on camp chairs and bus roofs, and Bella reappeared at Haylee's feet, tail flicking lazily, as if to say *told you so.*
Josie gave a soft huff and leaned into Haylee's leg, content.
They stayed there a while, just listening. The night air had cooled, and the fire threw long shadows that danced against the backs of vans and tents. Someone passed a pot of lentil stew around, and Haylee took a spoonful, savoring the smoky comfort of it. She hadn't expected to feel this at ease with people she'd only just met—but something about the festival stripped away the usual layers. No one here asked what you did for work. No one asked where you were headed next. It was enough that

you were here, breathing, present.

Later, she wandered back to Bertha alone. Isaac had given her a small piece of raw clay, pressed into her palm with a wink. "Something to mold when you're stuck. Just keep your hands busy." Inside the RV, she lit her little reading light and curled into bed, Bella stretching long beside her, Josie settling onto the floor with a sigh. The night was still alive outside—laughter, a guitar strum, the occasional howl of a coyote far off in the hills—but inside Bertha, there was calm. A cocoon of warmth and knowing. Haylee reached for her journal, ran her fingers over the cover, and then set it down
without opening it.
Not everything needed to be written yet. Some moments were meant to just be.

She closed her eyes and thought about Aggie. About the map. About all the places she hadn't yet seen, and all the versions of herself she hadn't yet met. And for the first time in what felt like forever, she didn't feel behind or broken or lost.
She just felt ready.
Ready for morning. Ready for the next town. Ready for the uncertainty.
And ready, most of all, to keep becoming.

Chapter 13:
Freedom, Found in Strangers

The next morning, Haylee woke to the crisp high-desert air and the distant call of birds echoing through the trees. The campground was still asleep, save for a few early risers sipping coffee beside their fire pits or quietly stretching in the sun. The sky stretched wide and cloudless—an endless canvas of possibility.

She poured herself a mug of coffee and stepped outside with Josie to explore the edges of the camp, letting the rhythm of morning settle into her bones. The gravel crunched beneath her boots, Josie trotting at her side with ears perked and alert. The breeze was soft, tugging at the hem of her sweatshirt, and for a brief, perfect moment, Haylee just was. No timelines. No inbox. Just breath, space, and the feeling of her own body moving through a quiet world.

She thought of her old mornings—how they always felt rushed, reactive. Her feet hitting the ground already in defense mode. But here? Everything had slowed. She could feel herself arriving more fully in her own skin, one quiet sunrise at a time.

Back at the site, Bertha stood content and still. Breakfast sizzled in her pan—eggs, avocado, leftover roasted potatoes from the night before. Bella emerged from the warmth of the bed just long enough to inspect the noise before curling again in a patch of sunlight.

Haylee stirred the pan, humming softly, when the crunch of footsteps on gravel caught her attention.

"Morning," came a low voice. "You mind if I join you?"

Startled, she turned to see a man about her age—late thirties, maybe early forties—with a weathered backpack and a tired kindness in his eyes. His jeans were dusty, his boots worn through the sole, but his smile was open and easy.

Josie rose instantly, tense but silent. Haylee's hand went instinctively to her head.

"Sure," she said after a beat. "I don't have much, but I've got coffee if you want it."

He nodded gratefully. "I'll never say no to coffee."

Haylee handed him a chipped enamel mug and motioned toward a folding camp chair. He sat down with a groan, stretching long legs toward the fire pit, Josie still seated like a sentinel between them.

"I'm Luke," he said, sipping the brew and making a face. "Damn. That's strong."

She laughed. "Gets the job done."

"I've been on the road for a couple months now," he said. "Mostly hitching.

Working odd jobs. You?"

"About a week," she replied. "Still figuring it out."

Luke tilted his head. "You don't look like someone who just left everything behind."

Haylee raised a brow. "What do I look like?"

He smiled. "Like someone who's starting to remember who she is."

That silenced her. Not in a bad way—but in that way you go still when someone names something you hadn't even realized was true yet.

They ate in easy quiet. Josie eventually settled between them, no longer on alert. The kind of calm that only comes when two people don't feel the need to fill the air with noise.

After a while, Luke spoke again, quieter this time. "People think freedom's about going wherever you want. But real freedom, I think, is about what you're willing to leave behind."

Haylee let the words hang there.

He continued, "You ever carry something so long you forgot you had a choice to put it down?"

She nodded, her throat tight. "Yeah. I carried a whole life that wasn't mine."

"Most of us do," he said, not unkindly. "Until one day we wake up and ask, 'What would happen if I just... let go?'"

She looked at him then—really looked. Not in a romantic way, but with the sudden respect that blooms when you realize you're speaking to someone who's already walked through a fire you've only just stepped into.

"I didn't realize how heavy it was until I left," she said.

Luke smiled. "Then you're already freer than most."

They talked for hours. About places they'd been, the people they'd trusted and the ones they'd had to let go of. He told her about working on a ranch in Montana, about a sister he hadn't spoken to in years, about the tattoo on his wrist that was once a wedding date and now just a faded scar.

"I still don't have it figured out," he said, stretching. "But the road makes space for that."

When the sun dipped low behind the trees, Luke stood and brushed dust from his pants.

"I should head out," he said, lifting his pack. "I've got a few more miles in me today."

Haylee nodded. "Thanks... for the company and honesty."

He smiled. "Thanks for the fire. And for letting a stranger sit in your peace."

He turned to leave, but then paused.

"You'll find it, you know. Whatever it is you're looking for. As long as you stay honest with yourself."

And then he was gone, swallowed by the trees and fading light.

Haylee stood there long after he disappeared, the weight of the day settling into something solid and grounding. She looked down at Josie, who had already curled up again by the fire, and then up at the sky turning dusky lavender above her.

Luke was right.

The road itself wasn't freedom. It was the invitation to let go, to listen, to notice what you no longer needed.

And for the first time in a long, long while, she didn't feel alone.

She felt ready.

Haylee left the Mirage Festival with her new journal full of poems, her heart full of quiet joy, and—for the first time in a long time—a clear sense of direction. Both literal and emotional. She had mapped a slow, mindful route north, planning to camp at a quiet BLM site near a canyon overlook Isaac had recommended.

Josie snoozed in the passenger seat, her paws twitching in a dream. Bella had taken up her new favorite spot curled in the RV's sink, blissfully indifferent to every bump in the road.

Haylee hummed to the mixtape she'd made from festival performances, her elbow resting out the window, letting the wind tangle her hair. The open road stretched ahead like a welcome mat. She felt good.

Which, of course, is when everything started to unravel.

First came a sputter.

Then a cough.

Then Bertha—a loyal beast with quirks Haylee had grown to love—lurched, shuddered, and rolled to a dead stop on a sunbaked stretch of two-lane highway with nothing in sight but mesquite brush and mirages.

Haylee blinked. "No, no, no... Come on, old girl. Don't do this to me now."

She turned the key. Click. Nothing. Just silence.

Bertha, once charmingly grumpy, now sat mute and defiant.

No cell service. No shade. The temperature climbing past ninety. The nearest sign of life miles behind her. The reality hit hard and fast: she was stranded in the middle of nowhere.

Josie picked up on her tension and began pacing the floor. Bella meowed once, unimpressed, then crawled beneath the passenger seat like a cat-shaped resignation.

Haylee sat in the driver's seat, breathing fast, her fingers gripping the wheel. Panic bubbled up, loud and uninvited. Tears welled. Her mind spun into that familiar spiral:

What if it's the alternator? What if I need a tow and there's no one for miles? What if this was a mistake? What if I'm not cut out for this?

She closed her eyes.

Took a breath.

Another.

She remembered what her aunt used to say: "Don't run from the moment. Stand in it. Even if it's messy."

So she stood in it. Literally. She stepped out, popped the hood, and stared at the mess of hoses and metal like it might give her a clue.

"All right, Bertha," she muttered, sweat trailing down her spine. "Let's figure this out together."

Two hours passed. No signal.

No passing cars. She drank water in careful sips, drew "HELP" in chalk rocks along the roadside, and weighed whether she should start walking or stay put.

Then—dust. A cloud forming in the distance. A vehicle. Her heart jumped.

A large fifth-wheel camper rumbled into view and slowed as it approached. Out stepped an older couple: Ken, sun-leathered and cheerful, and Nora, with a braid down her back and the kind of calm you only earn from years on the road.

"You okay, hon?" Nora asked, already holding out a bottle of water.

"I think it's the alternator," Haylee said, trying not to sound as small as she felt. "And I've got no signal."

"Well, you've got us," Ken grinned. "And a working satellite phone."

They helped her call a tow from the nearest outpost—a dusty little town called Shiloh Flats, population maybe a dozen on a busy weekend. While they waited, Nora shared stories over apples and peanut butter. They even offered space in their camper for her and the pets to rest in the A/C until help arrived.

"Most folks out here look out for each other," Nora said gently. "It's part of the code."

By sundown, Bertha was loaded onto a flatbed and hauled into Shiloh. The mechanic shop was no-frills—a tin-roofed garage with a stray dog in the shade and a sleepy-eyed man named Tom who confirmed what she feared: the alternator was toast.

"Not a hard fix," Tom said. "But I've gotta order the part. You'll be here two nights, maybe three."

Haylee nodded, masking the pinch in her chest. She wasn't upset with him. She was upset with herself—for letting a small setback feel like failure.

But then, something shifted.

Maybe it was the quiet of Shiloh Flats, or the way the locals waved without asking questions. Maybe it was the heat forcing her to slow down. She wandered the town's few blocks, met a woman named Della who ran both the post office and the bakery from the same counter. Later, she stumbled into an impromptu community potluck at a park made from two picnic tables and a rusted windmill. Someone handed her a paper plate stacked with potato salad and peach cobbler, and she sat beside a teenage girl who was crying over a broken backpack zipper.

Haylee fixed it with duct tape and a safety pin. They ended up talking for an hour—about writing, about what it means to feel lost, about the strange relief of being somewhere small enough to feel seen.

When Bertha was finally ready, Haylee didn't rush to leave.

She sat outside the shop for a while, scribbling in her journal with Bella on her lap and Josie stretched out in the dust beside her.

"The road isn't all sunrises and open mic nights, she wrote. *Sometimes it's busted bolts and busted plans. Sometimes it's sweat and silence and strangers who offer their shade without asking for anything in return. Just remember things happen FOR you, NOT to you."*

She closed the journal, her fingers tracing the weather-softened leather she had bartered for.

Before she climbed behind the wheel, she looked around at Shiloh Flats one more time. Not just the town—but the reminder. The lesson.

Freedom wasn't about flawless days. It was about learning to bend without breaking. To ask for help when you need it. To find family, even if only for a moment, in the most unexpected places.

That night, as Bertha rolled quietly out of town and the stars returned overhead, Haylee whispered a *thank-you* into the desert.

Not just for the fix.

But for the detour.

94

And in her journal, she scribbled before sleep:

"The road teaches you what freedom costs.
Sometimes, the price is patience.
Sometimes, humility.
Sometimes, a $300 alternator and a day without Wi-Fi."

Chapter 14:
The Next Step

The next few days blurred past in a steady rhythm of roads, rest stops, and reflection. Haylee woke early, made quiet breakfasts in the still hush of dawn, and drove until the sun dipped low behind unfamiliar hills. Each town offered its own flavor—quirky diners, silent main streets, friendly strangers—but none of them felt like home. Not yet.

With every mile, she felt more capable behind the wheel. She'd mastered the art of leveling Bertha on uneven terrain, brewing coffee in under five minutes, and finding public Wi-Fi without even trying. On paper, she was thriving.

But in the quiet spaces between the excitement, Haylee felt something else.

It was usually in the evenings—when the air cooled, campfires flickered in the distance, and the stars began their silent unveiling—that the ache crept in. A loneliness she hadn't expected. She had Josie and Bella, and that helped. But there was a deeper kind of connection she missed. The late-night talks, the spontaneous laughter, the simple comfort of feeling known. Even Jake, for all the chaos, had once filled that space.

She wasn't sure if it was grief or growth. Maybe both.

A few days later, at a gas station somewhere between desert nothingness and mountain air, she met Mia.

Mia's van was parked next to Bertha—a lived-in, paint-chipped old thing with a dreamcatcher dangling from the rearview. Mia herself looked like she'd stepped out of a travel documentary: sun-browned skin, wild curls, and a confidence that didn't need announcing.

Haylee was pumping gas when Mia strolled over, coffee in hand and mischief in her eyes.

"Hey," Mia said casually. "Mind if I borrow your trash can?"

Haylee laughed. "Help yourself. You need anything else while you're at it?"

"Just some of your good vibes," Mia winked, tossing her cup in and leaning casually on Bertha like they'd known each other for years.

There was something disarming about her—raw and real, like the kind of woman who didn't pretend to have it all figured out, but also wasn't afraid to keep moving forward anyway.

"Are you traveling alone?" Mia asked, nodding toward Haylee's setup.

"Just me, Josie, and Bella," Haylee said, scratching Josie behind the ears. "Been on the road a few weeks."

Mia smiled. "Love that. How's it been treating you?"

Haylee hesitated, then answered honestly. "It's been… freeing. But also kinda weird. I'm starting to realize how much I'd been living for other people."

Mia's expression softened. "I know that feeling. The road's like a mirror—it shows you who you are when no one's watching. Sometimes it's beautiful. Sometimes it's br utal."

Haylee nodded slowly. "Yeah. I thought I was escaping. But it turns out I was just… finding space. To finally think."

Mia tilted her head, a knowing glint in her eyes. "And to feel. That's the hardest part. But it's also the good part. Most people never give themselves that chance."

There was a long pause between them—comfortable, not awkward. Two travelers, somewhere between where they'd been and where they were going.

"You sound like you've been at this a while," Haylee said.

"Three years," Mia replied, tipping her head toward her van. "Left a cushy job, a relationship that wasn't right, and a version of myself I didn't like anymore. I didn't know what I was looking for. I still don't. But I've found pieces along the way."

Haylee smiled. "That gives me hope. I think I'm still in the undoing phase."

Mia grinned. "Undoing is where it starts. The rebuilding comes next. You don't have to rush it."

They exchanged numbers and a few campsite tips. When they parted, there were no promises—just a quiet understanding. A recognition between wanderers that the road sometimes gives you people exactly when you need them.

As Haylee pulled away from the station, Josie jumped into the co-pilot seat, tail wagging like she'd just had a conversation of her own. Bella blinked lazily from the dash.

Haylee looked out at the road ahead and whispered, "Let's be bolder."

The wind picked up, rustling the map on her dash.

Haylee wasn't sure how long she could keep driving before the weight of solitude caught up with her. Even with the girls by her side, some days the silence stretched too wide, too long.

That's when Amelia called.

Amelia had once been her loudest cheerleader—and her sharpest truth-teller. Their friendship had dimmed in the chaos of Haylee's former life: long hours, an unraveling relationship, and a version of herself she barely recognized.

But now, Amelia's voice burst through the speaker like a memory restored.

"So… you're really doing this?" she asked, half-laughing. "Six months? On the road? Alone?"

Haylee grinned. "Looks like it."

"I mean... damn, Hay. I always knew you had it in you. I'm proud of you. And also worried. But mostly proud."

They talked for over an hour. About how freeing it was to not know what came next. About fear. About the unexpected magic.

Before hanging up, Amelia said softly, "You don't have to do this alone. I'm still here, okay? Even if you're a thousand miles away."

Haylee's throat tightened. "Thank you. That means more than you know."

Not even ten minutes after the call ended, her phone buzzed again.

Jake.

Her stomach dropped.
Jake:

"You really just walked away from everything, huh? You're not cut out for this, Haylee. You need stability. You'll get tired of pretending. You always do."

His words landed like cold water.

But this time, something inside her didn't flinch. She read the message again, and instead of doubt, she felt resolve.

She opened the reply screen.

Haylee:
I'm not pretending. I'm growing. I'm not the version of me you kept trying to shrink. I'm not running—I'm finally standing still long enough to see who I really am. And I'm done letting you define that.

She hit send. Then blocked his number.

The wind picked up outside, brushing dust against the windshield. Josie stirred. Bella blinked.

Haylee sat back in her seat, her pulse loud in her ears. But it wasn't fear.

It was freedom.

She turned the key in Bertha's ignition. The engine rumbled to life.

As they pulled away from the rest stop, she whispered to herself, "I'm enough. I always was."

And with the road stretching ahead in a ribbon of light and dust, Haylee smiled.

She wasn't running anymore.
She was becoming.

Chapter 15:
Where the Wild Things Went

The day had been perfect. A calm, hazy afternoon by the lake—the kind of peaceful retreat Haylee had been craving. Josie spent the day running in and out of the shallows, her fur drying stiff in the heat. Bella, ever the queen of comfort, lounged on the dash with her eyes half-lidded in the late sun.

It was the kind of day that made Haylee feel like she was finally getting the hang of this life. Like the road was no longer about escape, but about finding her place.

Dinner was simple: pasta with vegetables while Josie chewed on a stick by the shore. Bella, naturally, had claimed the sink again like a throne.

But then, as the sky shifted to lavender and burnt orange, something changed.

Josie disappeared.

At first, it was subtle. Haylee noticed the familiar rustle of paws had gone quiet. When she looked over her shoulder, Josie wasn't there. Probably chasing a scent in the brush, Haylee thought.

"Josie, come on," she called casually. A low whistle, a few more words. Nothing unusual.

But seconds turned into minutes. And minutes stretched painfully thin.

"Josie!" she called again, louder now. The edge in her voice began to sharpen, shifting from playful to tense.

She stepped out of the RV into the cooling air, scanning the campsite. Still no sign.

"Come on, Josie. I don't have time for this."

She circled the area, shaking the treat bag that usually sent Josie running.

Still nothing. No bark. No flash of movement. No paws skittering toward her with joy.
Just silence.

Her stomach dropped.

This isn't good. Her heart pounded in her chest, each beat sharper than the last. She tried to swallow the panic, but it rose fast, hot and suffocating.

Josie was never gone this long.
Not without coming back.
Not like this.

Her thoughts spiraled.
What if she was stuck? Hurt?
What if something worse had happened?

The fear came on like fog—slow at first, then so thick she couldn't see past it. This was what she'd tried to leave behind. The helplessness. The weight of things beyond her control.

"Josie!" she yelled again, her voice cracking.

She hated how desperate it sounded. Too raw. Too real.
Wasn't she supposed to be stronger than this? The unflappable one, the woman who rolled with the punches and kept on driving? But right now, she was just a terrified woman in the middle of nowhere, calling into the dark for the only piece of home she had left.

She grabbed her flashlight, stumbling into the brush. The beam trembled in her hands, sweeping frantic arcs across the dark.
The desert night had settled thick and still, the silence pressing against her like a wall. No breeze. No insects. No movement. Just the sound of her own uneven breathing.

"Josie… please. Come back."
Her voice broke.

She sounded like someone lost. Someone unraveling.
And she hated that.
Hated how fragile it made her feel.
Like freedom had lied to her.

This wasn't an adventure. This was fear.

She kept calling, throat growing raw. Her flashlight flickered.
Don't do this, she told herself. Don't imagine the worst.
But she couldn't stop.
What if Josie was gone?
What if, in the middle of a perfect day, the best part of her life had slipped away?

A gust of wind stirred dust into her eyes. Her heart slammed in her chest, panic radiating outward until her knees felt weak.
She paused, forcing herself to breathe, to think.

But even then, all she wanted was someone else.
Someone steady. Someone who knew what to do.

She thought of Jake.
The longing surprised her. Not just for him—but for anyone. Someone to carry this with her. Someone to say, Hey. You're not alone.
She let out a bitter laugh, the sound strange and brittle in the dark.
But no one was there.
Just her, and her fear.

She wandered deeper, calling until her voice gave out. Her muscles ached. Her mind screamed.
She was so damn tired. Tired of being the one who held everything together. Tired of pretending she didn't feel fragile. Tired of doing it all alone.

And in that raw, unraveling moment, it hit her:
This—this fear, this vulnerability—was exactly what she had tried to outrun.

But the road didn't care. The road didn't wait.

She stood there, knees shaking, breath catching in her throat—
—and heard it.

A rustle in the brush. The soft thump of paws on dirt.

She froze.
"Josie?" she whispered.

And then, from the shadows—Josie.
Tail wagging, fur damp, eyes gleaming like she'd just returned from some grand escapade.

Relief hit Haylee like a wave. Her knees buckled, and she sank to the ground as Josie bounded toward her, licking her face as if to say, I'm here, Mom. What's the big deal?

Haylee laughed and cried all at once, burying her face in Josie's warm, wild fur. The panic melted into something softer—still intense, but no longer sharp.

"Where the hell did you go?" she whispered, her voice shaking. "You scared me so much."

Josie licked her again, tail wagging without shame.
And just like that, the night didn't feel so heavy.

Haylee held her close, breathing in the scent of wet fur and wild desert air. She wasn't alone. Not really.
And maybe, just maybe, it was okay to be fragile sometimes.

As Josie trotted a few feet away, tail high, Haylee watched her with a smile that ached from inside. There was something in the way she moved—free, unbothered—that said she hadn't been lost at all. Just exploring.
And now, she was back.

The relief swelled again, this time warmer, steadier. Haylee stumbled to her feet, laughing through a fresh wave of tears.

"Josie!" she choked out, opening her arms.

Josie barreled back into her, pressing her whole body against Haylee like she'd missed her too. Her tongue found Haylee's cheeks again, messy and eager.

"I missed you too," Haylee whispered, hugging her tight. "But you had the best time, didn't you?"

Josie wagged harder, tongue lolling, eyes bright.
"Absolutely", she seemed to say. But I came back. I always come back.

Haylee stroked her ears, smiling through tears, and felt the last of the fear ebb away. For all the chaos of the road, this—this connection—was her constant. Her anchor.

She reached for a treat bag, the crinkle catching Josie's attention instantly. Josie sat, eyes locked, tail a metronome of joy.
Haylee tossed a treat, and Josie snapped it from the air like a pro.

I got lost, but I didn't forget where home is.
And Haylee believed her.

The stars blinked to life above them. The last of the sun dipped behind the mountains, and the desert night settled again—but this time, it felt different.
It felt like peace.

With Josie curled up beside her, Haylee finally understood what she hadn't known she needed:
The road wasn't always about answers. Or healing. Or escape.
Sometimes it was just about presence.
About being here—in the messy, breathtaking moment.
And knowing someone would always find their way back.
For now, that was enough.

Chapter 16:
Redefining Love and Self

The days after meeting Mia were filled with contemplation for Haylee. She couldn't stop thinking about the woman who had spoken so confidently about her life on the road. It was as if Mia had given Haylee permission—permission to fully embrace the freedom that was just beginning to take root in her life.

But it wasn't just the idea of freedom that stuck with Haylee. It was the way Mia spoke about independence, about being true to herself, and about not needing anyone to validate her journey. It was a stark contrast to the life Haylee had lived with Jake—the codependent, toxic relationship where she had often sacrificed her own needs to make him happy, to keep him satisfied.

As much as Haylee had known deep down that breaking up with Jake had been the right choice, there were still moments where she doubted herself. Had she made the right decision? Was she simply running away from something harder to face?

That evening, after a long day of driving, Haylee found herself on the phone with her dad. Josie and Bella were curled up together on the bed, fast asleep.

"How's Bertha treating you?" her dad asked, his voice warm but distant. He never really understood the whole RV life, but he was trying to be supportive.

"It's going well," Haylee said quietly. "I'm settling in. I'm starting to figure things out, but..."

"But?"

"I don't know," she sighed, gazing out the window at the wide, starry sky above. "I've been thinking a lot about what Mia said the other day. She's been on the road for years, and she just... lives her life on her own terms. And I keep wondering if that's the kind of person I want to be. The kind of life I want to live."

"Sounds like you're having an epiphany," her dad said with a laugh, though there was a hint of concern in his voice.

"Yeah, maybe," Haylee replied softly. "But it's not just about the road anymore. It's about everything. About who I am and what I need."

Her dad was silent for a moment. "I know it's been tough since your mom passed, and it sounds like you're doing what's right for you. But don't be too hard on yourself. You don't have to have it all figured out right now."

"I know," she replied, her voice growing firmer. "But I think I've been avoiding some things. Not just the past, but... who I am. What I want in my life, what I want out of relationships. I spent so long trying to make Jake happy, to make him okay, that I lost myself. I'm scared I've forgotten how to be me."

Her dad sighed deeply. "I get it, kiddo. But the fact that you're asking yourself these questions means you're moving forward. Just keep going. Take your time. No one's in a hurry."

The conversation ended with more words of encouragement, but Haylee didn't feel much better. She'd learned a lot from the past few months on the road. It was clear she was growing, but there was still a part of her that held onto the idea of love as something she needed to find, something she needed to complete her. She had this lingering thought that maybe, just maybe, she could go back to Jake. After all, they had a history. Ten years, in fact. Wasn't there some kind of redemption or reconciliation possible?

The thought seemed to linger as Haylee stared out at the night sky, her phone still in her hand. She glanced at Josie and Bella, curled up together, and smiled. This was what it was all about—our journey. It wasn't just Haylee's journey anymore; they were a family, and they were in this together.

In that moment, she realized the truth: what she needed wasn't to go back to her old life, or to fall into the familiar comforts of a relationship that no longer served her. What she needed was to rediscover her own sense of self.

The next day, as she was passing through a small mountain town, the decision was made for her.

Jake's name popped up on her phone.

Haylee hesitated before answering, a mix of curiosity and dread welling up inside her. What could he possibly want now?

"Hello?" Haylee's voice was cautious.

"Hey, Haylee," Jake's voice was warm, but there was a familiar edge to it. "I've been thinking. I know we haven't talked in a while, but... I miss you."

There it was. The words she had been both expecting and dreading. The ones that always made her second-guess herself. Looking over at Josie, then back at the road ahead, Haylee took a deep breath.

"I don't think we need to talk about this, Jake," she replied, her voice steady. "We've been down this road before, and it didn't end well. I've moved on. I'm not the same person I was when we were together."

"Come on, Hay," he coaxed, his tone shifting. "You and I both know we were good together. I've changed. I've realized a lot of things. Why don't you just come back? We can figure things out."

Her chest tightened, and she glanced at the landscape around her—tall, sweeping trees and a wide-open sky that felt endless. At that moment, she knew what she had to do. It wasn't just about saying goodbye to Jake—it was about saying goodbye to the part of herself that had clung to him out of fear.

"I'm not coming back, Jake," she said firmly, her words cutting through the silence. "I'm living my own life now. I'm finding out who I am, and I can't do that with you holding me back. I wish you well, but this... it's over."

The silence on the other end of the line stretched out, and for a moment, Haylee thought he might protest, beg her to reconsider. But instead, he simply said, "Okay, Haylee. I hope you're happy."

The call ended, and Haylee sat in the driver's seat of Bertha, her fingers still on the phone. There was no rush of relief or triumph, just a quiet sense of peace. A feeling of finally releasing something that had held her back for so long. She looked at Josie, who was sitting up, her eyes wide with concern.

"It's alright, Josie. We're alright now," Haylee murmured, rubbing her dog's ear gently. Josie hesitated for a moment before turning to watch the passing vehicles, and Haylee couldn't help but smile.

As she continued on her journey, Haylee realized that she had just taken another step toward becoming the person she had always wanted to be. She wasn't defined by her past anymore, or by relationships she had outgrown. The road was teaching her to be her own source of fulfillment, to redefine what love and happiness meant on her own terms.

Trusting Her Instincts

Haylee had been parked at the small, dusty campground for two nights. The place was quiet at first, nestled along a forgotten highway, far from the tourist crowds, with only a handful of RVs scattered across the lot. The sun was low in the sky, casting long shadows over the gravel paths.

Josie had settled into her routine of lounging in the driver's seat, keeping an eye out for the occasional squirrel or passing car. Bella, as usual, was curled up in a small nook by the kitchen window, her golden eyes blinking lazily.

It was supposed to be peaceful.

But that was before they showed up.

The first sign of trouble was the two men. They parked their truck too close to Bertha, the engine growling as they shifted it into place. Haylee didn't think much of it at first—they looked like travelers, maybe passing through—but something about the way they looked at her made her skin crawl.

One of them, tall with a thick beard, walked past her RV without so much as a glance. The other, shorter and wiry, stared directly into her windows as he passed, his eyes lingering just a bit too long.

Haylee stiffened. She wasn't paranoid, but the air around her shifted. It was that gut feeling she couldn't ignore. Her intuition told her they weren't just passing through.

As dusk settled into night, the two men lingered by their truck, talking in low voices, their conversation punctuated by occasional laughter. They seemed to be waiting for something... or someone.

Haylee had learned over the years to listen to that little voice in her head—the one that wasn't always logical, but always right. It told her when something felt off, when she was in danger, when she needed to get out of a situation. She'd started ignoring it in the past, but not anymore.

Josie, ever the perceptive companion, was now on alert, her tail twitching at the slightest sound. Bella, meanwhile, had shifted to sit in the window, her eyes narrowing as she stared at the men with the intensity of a hunter.

Haylee took a deep breath and glanced around. The campground was small, and the nearest neighbor was at least a hundred yards away. Not much help if something went wrong.

"Alright, Josie," she muttered, her heart racing slightly. "We're leaving. Now."

She grabbed her keys and quickly gathered her things, keeping an eye on the men. They hadn't moved closer, but Haylee couldn't shake the feeling they were sizing her up, planning something she wasn't interested in being a part of.

Haylee didn't hesitate. She slipped into the driver's seat, started the engine, and carefully backed out of her spot, driving away slowly enough to not draw attention, but fast enough to make it to the exit before anyone could follow.

As she drove down the road, Josie's head popped up from the passenger seat, ears alert, scanning for any sign of pursuit. Bella remained quiet in her usual spot, a picture of calm.

Even though she was driving away, Haylee's heart still raced. She replayed the situation in her mind. What if she hadn't listened? What if she had stayed?

But no. Trust yourself. You're not just wandering aimlessly. You know exactly what to do.

She kept driving, heading toward a nearby state park she had seen on her map. The road ahead felt clearer now, her decision more resolute. It was time to take control, to follow her instincts, to take her safety—and her life—seriously.

The park was smaller, tucked between hills and lined with quiet walking trails. It was late, and the campground was nearly empty, save for a few RVs around the perimeter. She found a quiet spot, well away from the main path, and settled in.

Haylee let out a breath she didn't realize she was holding. It felt good to be away from the tension, away from the unwanted presence of those men. She had made a decision that had saved her, though she wasn't sure from what exactly.

After setting up camp, she decided to clear her head with a walk. As she strolled along the trail, she passed a group of RVers sitting around a campfire, talking and laughing, the faint strumming of a guitar rising in the air.

One of them, a woman with short red hair and a warm smile, waved at her. "Hey! You look like you could use a little company. We're just getting started with some s'mores. Wanna join us?"

Haylee hesitated for only a moment. She wasn't used to this kind of openness from strangers, but something about the woman's welcoming energy put her at ease.

"Sure, I'd love to."

As she walked over, the group immediately made space for her. There was an older couple in their 60s, traveling full-time in a renovated school bus; a middle-aged man with a passion for hiking and photography; and the woman with the guitar, who introduced herself as Maya.

They shared stories of the road, laughed over marshmallows, and spoke of their journeys. There was a lightheartedness to the conversation, a sense of belonging that Haylee hadn't realized she needed until now.

"You know," Maya said, "I can't tell you how many people come out here and think they're doing it for the 'wrong' reasons. They doubt themselves all the time—think they're running away from something instead of running toward something. But the road? The road is about finding yourself, not escaping who you were."

Haylee smiled, feeling a weight lift from her chest. "That's exactly it. I think I've been afraid to admit that I was always running from something. But now... now I'm doing it because I want to. Because I deserve this."

"You do deserve it," Maya said firmly. "We all do.

No matter where we come from, what we've been through. We're all just people trying to find our way."

Haylee's heart swelled. For the first time in a long time, she felt like she was exactly where she was supposed to be.

Chapter 17:
New Horizons

The days following her conversation with Jake felt noticeably lighter. Haylee moved through them with a quiet kind of peace, a release she hadn't realized she needed until she felt it settle in her chest. Letting go of the past didn't mean the doubts or insecurities vanished completely—she knew the road wouldn't always be smooth—but something had shifted. Taking ownership of her life, her choices, her future… it made everything feel just a little more possible.

One early morning, with the campground still hushed and the sky painted in soft amber tones, Haylee decided to take Bertha into a nearby town. The sun stretched low over the horizon, casting golden light on the sleepy landscape. Everything about the morning felt like a beginning.

As she drove along a winding dirt road, a small café caught her eye. It was tucked into the corner of the town square, its brick façade worn but full of charm, with ivy climbing up the side like nature itself had claimed it. It practically called to her. She pulled into the lot and glanced at Josie.
"What do you think, girl?" she asked. Josie perked up and peered out the window, as if giving her nod of approval.

They stepped out into the cool air, both stretching as though the road had weighed heavy on their limbs. After a short walk around the block, Josie seemed content to return to the RV. Haylee, however, followed the scent of roasted beans and buttery pastries into the café.

Inside, the place wrapped around her like a warm hug. Soft music drifted from overhead, and the clinking of mugs and the low murmur of conversation created a kind of stillness that felt like home. Behind the counter stood a man—late thirties, tall, with shaggy brown hair and an easy smile. There was something calming about him, a presence that felt grounded, like someone who didn't need to rush.

"What can I get for you this morning?" he asked, his tone relaxed.

"Just a black coffee, please," Haylee said, offering a small smile.

He poured her drink with a steady hand. "You passing through?"

She nodded. "Been on the road for a few months now. Trying to figure things out."

"Aren't we all," he said, with a knowing tilt of his head. "The road's good for that—clears the noise."

Haylee took her coffee and leaned against the counter for a moment, feeling the weight of his words. She didn't usually linger, didn't usually open up to strangers. But there was something in the way he spoke—unrushed, sincere—that made her stay a little longer.

"I used to think I had everything figured out," she said quietly. "Turns out I was just following a script someone else wrote for me."

He smiled. "Yeah. A lot of us do. Until we realize we can toss that script."

A beat of silence passed between them, comfortable and unhurried.

"I'm Sam, by the way."

"Haylee."

"Well, Haylee," Sam said, with a teasing glint in his eye, "if you ever need a break from all that soul-searching, we've got good coffee and I make a mean breakfast bur rito."

She laughed. It was easy, genuine. "I'll keep that in mind."

As she left the café, notebook in hand, she felt the kind of smile that didn't fade quickly. Not a spark, a reminder that new beginnings sometimes start with good coffee and a kind voice.

The next few days blurred in a rhythm of travel and reflection. Small towns came and went, each one offering something new—a fresh path, a quiet moment, a new face.

But something about Sam's quiet presence stayed with her. It wasn't about him, exactly. It was the reminder that kindness existed in unexpected places, and that maybe the road didn't have to be lonely to be freeing.

One morning, parked in the serenity of a hidden forest clearing, Haylee sat with her aunt's journal open in her lap. The pages, filled with decades-old musings from a woman who had once chased the same freedom, had become her compass. She read an entry about standing still—about learning when the journey wasn't about movement, but about listening.

It made her pause. She had come so far. The renovations. The late nights of doubt. The quiet victories. And now this—an unexpected peace in the not knowing. The space she had created wasn't just in Bertha. It was in her heart, too.

But that morning, as the breeze whispered through the trees and the soft rustle of leaves filled the space around her, she let a question rise to the surface: What's next? Not because she needed an answer, but because she was ready to start asking.

Her life had changed in ways she never could have planned. And for the first time, Haylee wasn't looking for certainty. She was looking forward to it.

Haylee closed the journal and stood to stretch, breathing in the scent of pine and earth. Josie padded over and nudged her leg, tail wagging softly.
"Alright, girl," Haylee said with a small laugh. "Let's hit the road. See what's waiting for us."

She packed up slowly, methodically, the way she always did when she didn't want to rush a good morning. Everything about the day felt open, full of potential. She was humming as she slid into the driver's seat and turned the key.

Bertha rumbled to life.

Haylee pulled out onto the narrow road leading away from the clearing, the sun warm on her face, a soft breeze coming through the open window. She reached for her phone to check the map.
One new notification.

Unknown Number: *"You might want to be careful who you trust out there."*

Her fingers tightened around the phone. The breeze suddenly felt colder. Josie stirred in the passenger seat, sensing the shift in energy.
Haylee's heart thudded.

She read the message again.
And again.

Then she looked out at the winding road ahead—wide open, but now laced with shadows.

Chapter 18:
Wisdom on the Road

Haylee was halfway through her morning routine, drinking a cup of coffee and watching the mist rise over the distant hills, when she spotted her: a young woman in her twenties, confidently unrolling a yoga mat beside a vintage van with a sun-bleached mural of mountains painted on the side. Her van was parked just a few spaces down from Haylee, and she seemed to be setting up a peaceful, zen-like morning, stretching in the soft light of dawn.

Haylee, curious, put down her coffee mug and walked over to introduce herself. The young woman looked up with a smile, clearly comfortable in her own skin. She had an air of easy confidence—something Haylee was still working on.

"Hey there," Haylee called out, her voice hesitant but warm.

The woman stood up, brushing off her yoga pants and offering a hand. "Morning! I'm Zoe."

"Haylee," she replied, shaking Zoe's hand. "Nice to meet you."

"I saw you parked here last night," Zoe said, glancing at Haylee's RV. "Nice rig. How's the road treating you so far?"

Haylee smiled, glad to be talking to someone who seemed down-to-earth. "It's been good, but... I'm still adjusting. Traveling solo, you know? There are a few things I'm still figuring out."

Zoe nodded knowingly. "Yeah, I get that. It's a big transition. I've been on the road for about two years now, so I've picked up a few things along the way. Wanna grab some breakfast? I've got some pancakes going."

Haylee, eager for any advice Zoe might have, gladly accepted. The two women sat together outside Zoe's van, sharing pancakes and coffee. As the sun climbed higher, the conversation turned toward safety—something that was always in the back of Haylee's mind but hadn't quite been addressed in a practical way until now.

The Solo Traveler's Survival Guide

"So, how do you manage, being out here alone and all?" Haylee asked, taking a bite of her pancake. Zoe chewed thoughtfully for a moment, then set down her plate.

"First thing's first, you've gotta trust your gut. Your intuition is one of your best tools out here. If something feels off, it probably is."

Haylee nodded, remembering the unsettling feeling she'd had with those men at the last campground. She wasn't sure if they'd intended to harm her, but something about them had felt dangerous.

Zoe continued, "But it's also about perception. You can't always tell what a situation will turn into, but you can make it clear to others that you're not alone. I always make sure my van looks a little more 'occupied' than it actually is. Add a couple of chairs outside, and maybe a few items that suggest I've got someone with me. It's all about the little things that make you appear less of a target."

Haylee raised an eyebrow. "Like what, exactly?"

"Two camping chairs," Zoe said with a grin. "Old, worn-in ones. You can find them at thrift stores. Make it look like you've got a buddy or someone staying with you."

Haylee's eyes widened with realization. It was so simple, but it made total sense.

"And don't forget the boots," Zoe added, her voice light but serious. "Get a pair of men's boots—old, like they've seen a lot of use. You don't need to wear them, just leave them out by the door, like someone's been around recently. Makes it look like you've got company."

Haylee laughed at the thought, but there was something comforting about Zoe's calm, practical approach to safety.

"Also, don't underestimate the power of bear spray," Zoe continued.

"I keep mine right next to the door. You never know what kind of wildlife you'll run into—or even people, sometimes. I know it sounds paranoid, but you'd rather be safe than sorry."

Haylee nodded again, filing away these tips. She hadn't thought about the little things that could make a big difference in her sense of security.

"And what about at night?" Haylee asked. "I mean, it can feel a little... vulnerable, sleeping out here by yourself. I know I've had some restless nights thinking about worst-case scenarios."

Zoe's expression softened. "I get it. Honestly, I still have moments where I wake up in the middle of the night and feel like I'm not alone. But one thing that really helps is keeping your keys beside your bed. That way, if you need to leave quickly, you're not fumbling around for them in the dark."

Haylee looked surprised. "That's actually brilliant."

"Right?" Zoe said with a wink. "It's just one of those little tricks to make sure you stay calm and collected. In an emergency, your head's already spinning, so you need to be prepared. Keep a level head and remember: if something goes wrong, don't panic. Easier said than done, but if you can remain calm, you'll be able to think clearly."

"Thank you for all this," Haylee said, feeling more empowered than she had in a while. "I think I was so focused on all the big stuff—getting Bertha ready, finding places to park—that I didn't think about the little details that could make all the difference."

"Anytime," Zoe replied, leaning back on her hands, her eyes sparkling with the confidence of someone who'd been there, done that. "You'll get the hang of it. Just trust yourself. The road's full of surprises, and it's all part of the journey. Don't doubt yourself. And remember, you've got everything you need right inside you."

Chapter 19:
The Rally

Several months after that first conversation with Zoe, Haylee had grown more confident on the road. Her mornings now started with a quick walk with Josie and Bella, followed by a little journaling or reading before setting off for the day's adventures. She'd met more solo travelers along the way, each with their own story, their own reasons for living on the road, and they'd shared tips, laughter, and the occasional offbeat potluck or campfire.

One afternoon, as she was cleaning up after a stop at a quiet national park, Haylee received a text that made her smile. It was from Zoe.

Zoe: "Hey, Haylee! I know it's been a while, but I just found out about this RV travelers' rally happening next month in Arizona. It's for solo travelers, people who've been on the road for at least six months. You in?"

Haylee smiled at the message. After all the time she'd spent alone on the road, meeting Zoe in that park felt like a small miracle. She hadn't expected to stay in touch with anyone so consistently, but Zoe had proven to be a good friend and mentor, and Haylee was eager to catch up.

Haylee: *"That sounds amazing! I'm definitely in. Would love to see you again."*

The rally was a few weeks away, but Haylee was already planning. She'd traveled through Arizona a few months back, but she'd never stopped for longer than a quick overnight rest. Now, the thought of meeting up with other solo travelers—of connecting with more people who understood her journey—felt like just what she needed.

When Haylee finally pulled into the BLM land where the rally was being held, she was taken aback by the sea of campers and RVs. The event was bigger than she had imagined—hundreds of rigs scattered across the park, each one filled with stories and adventures of people just like her. From vintage buses to sleek trailers, the variety of vehicles was endless, and she couldn't help but feel a sense of belonging.

She parked Bertha, set up her usual camp, and immediately texted Zoe to let her know she had arrived.

Minutes later, a familiar figure appeared, waving enthusiastically from across the park. Zoe's energy was infectious as she jogged over to Haylee, a wide grin on her face. Haylee met her with a warm hug.

"You made it!" Zoe exclaimed, her voice filled with excitement.

"Of course! I wouldn't miss this for the world," Haylee said, laughing. "It's crazy how many people are here."

"I know!" Zoe replied. "There are so many solo travelers, and they all have such different stories. It's kind of like a big family reunion for nomads. Come on, let me show you around."

Zoe led Haylee through the rally grounds, pointing out various booths with information about RV upgrades, boondocking tips, off-grid living, and even live music. There were fire pits where people gathered to share stories and impromptu potlucks happening in almost every corner.

As the afternoon wore on, Haylee found herself chatting with a few other solo travelers. They swapped tips on everything from managing finances on the road to keeping up with regular maintenance. Haylee could see how this lifestyle had forged a new kind of connection between people—an understanding that didn't need words, just shared experiences.

As the sun dipped low, casting a golden hue over the rally, Haylee and Zoe found a quieter spot by a small creek to sit and talk. It had been an incredible day—one filled with laughter, new friends, and a sense of solidarity. For the first time in a long while, Haylee felt like she was truly part of something bigger than herself.

"So, how's the journey been since we last talked?" Zoe asked, pulling out a small notebook from her bag.

Haylee took a deep breath, feeling a mixture of excitement and gratitude. "It's been amazing, actually. There have been some hard moments, but I feel like I'm finally living on my own terms. I've learned so much about myself—and about what I really want out of life."

"I knew you'd get there," Zoe said, her voice warm. "It's not always easy, but the road has a way of showing you things you'd never expect."

Haylee smiled. "I think I'm ready for whatever comes next, honestly. I've had my moments of doubt, but the more I travel, the more I realize that this—this freedom—is what I've been looking for."

Zoe nodded in understanding. "You're doing great. Just keep listening to yourself. And remember, you're never really alone out here. There's always someone who gets it."

Later that evening, after the sun had set and the stars had begun to twinkle overhead, a spontaneous open mic event kicked off near the main fire pit. Haylee was a little hesitant at first, but Zoe nudged her playfully.

"You know you're welcome to join in if you want," Zoe said, a teasing grin on her face. "I think you could tell some pretty great stories from your travels."

Haylee laughed, the thought of performing making her a little nervous. But there was something about the spirit of the rally, the supportive environment, that made her feel brave.

"I'll think about it," Haylee said, feeling the stirrings of something she hadn't felt in a long time: confidence.

That night, under a blanket of stars, Haylee sat by the fire with her new friends. The uncertainty of her past was slowly melting away, and in its place was a new sense of purpose. She was no longer the person she'd been when she first stepped into Bertha. She had grown, faced her fears, and learned to trust the journey, even when the road ahead was unclear.

Zoe, noticing Haylee's thoughtful expression, leaned over and gave her a small nudge. "Hey, you're doing great. Don't forget that, okay?"

Haylee smiled, grateful for the reminder. "I won't. Thank you, Zoe."

Chapter 20:
The Open Road

Even after Haylee talked with Zoe, she couldn't shake the eerie feeling she had after she received that anonymous text a few days earlier.

The sun had just crested the horizon, casting a soft golden hue across the landscape. Haylee was parked at a quiet campground on the outskirts of a small town, nestled beside a calm river. The air was cool and clean, scented with pine and damp earth, and the gentle rush of water over rocks was steady and soothing. Mornings like this reminded Haylee why she chose this life—free, untethered, and brimming with promise.

She stood outside Bertha, a steaming mug of coffee warming her hands, staring out at the river while Josie sniffed along the grass nearby. Peaceful as it was, a restlessness stirred inside her. The road never stopped moving—and neither did she. But lately, she'd started to wonder: Was she running toward something, or still away from something else?

A few days later, she found herself folding laundry at an RV park's coin-operated facility, letting her mind drift, when her phone buzzed. She wiped her hands on a towel and checked the screen.

Dad

Haylee, I need to talk to you. Call me when you get a chance.

Her stomach tightened. Her father rarely reached out—and never without a reason. They'd barely spoken since she left, just a few clipped conversations and polite updates. This message felt... different. Ominous.

She called immediately, heart pounding.

"Dad?"

"Haylee." His voice was thick, hesitant. "I've been doing a lot of thinking... about your aunt. About your mom. About... you.

I haven't been much of a father, and I know that. But I want to fix things. I want to come see you."

The words hit harder than she expected. It had been years since he made any move to be involved in her life beyond the bare minimum. Now, he wanted to visit? To talk?

"Dad, I..." she faltered. "That's a lot to process."

"I get that," he said quickly. "I don't expect anything. But there's something I need to talk to you about. Something that should've been said a long time ago. I'd rather do it face-to-face."

Haylee stood in silence, holding the phone as if it weighed a hundred pounds. She had worked so hard to build a new life, to heal. Could she really open the door to someone who'd left her to pick up all the broken pieces alone?

"I'm not the same person anymore," she said at last, her voice quiet. "I've built something here. I don't know if I'm ready to let you in."

"I understand," he said. "But I'm coming. I need to make this right. I just hope... you'll hear me out."

A long silence followed.
"Okay," she whispered. "Come. But no promises."

"I'll see you soon."

When the call ended, Haylee sat motionless, the hum of the laundry machines suddenly too loud. Her mind reeled with questions she couldn't answer.
Why now? What was he hiding? What had he never told her? That night, she sat by the campfire with Josie curled at her feet and Bella watching fireflies from her perch on the folding chair. Haylee sipped her tea, her thoughts drifting like smoke into the night sky.

The stars blinked above her, vast and silent.

She had no idea what her father's arrival would bring. But the sense of finality in his voice unsettled her more than she wanted to admit.

Just as she stood to go inside, her phone buzzed again.

A new message.

Not from her father.

Unknown number: *"You think you know everything, Haylee. But you don't. Be careful who you trust."*

Haylee stared at the screen, pulse quickening. Josie let out a low growl.

The fire crackled behind her, but the warmth was gone.
The open road no longer felt so wide.

Chapter 21:
Confronting the Past

A week had passed since the call from her father, and Haylee had done everything she could to stay grounded—journaling, walking Josie, distracting herself with camp chores. But when the knock came on Bertha's door that evening, it sent a jolt through her chest. She hadn't expected him to arrive so soon.

She set down her mug of tea and glanced at the clock. Outside, the sun was dipping below the horizon, casting long shadows across the gravel campground. Josie stood alert, ears perked.

Haylee took a breath and opened the door.

There he was. Her father. Suitcase in one hand, uncertainty in his eyes, wearing a hesitant smile that didn't quite reach his face.

"Dad," she said softly, unsure what emotion should come next.

"I hope I'm not interrupting," he said, shifting his weight. "I wasn't sure you'd want me to just... show up."

"I wasn't expecting you so soon," she replied honestly, stepping aside. "But come in."

He entered slowly, eyes scanning the small space as if trying to make sense of this new version of her life. "It's cozier than I imagined," he said, though his tone was more curious than critical.

"It works for me," she said, her smile tight. "It's still a work in progress."

He crouched to greet Josie, who gave Haylee a cautious look before leaning in for a sniff. Just then, Bella padded down from the dash and flicked her tail disapprovingly as she passed.

They sat at the dinette, the space between them filled with years of silence. Finally, her father spoke.

"I've been thinking a lot about you. About your mom." His voice had softened, but it still carried the weight of old guilt.

Haylee looked away, her throat tightening. "It's a little late for that, don't you think?"

"I know it is," he said quickly. "And I won't pretend I can undo the past. I just... I want to be part of your life again. If you'll let me."

She stared at him, her pulse quickening. She wanted to believe him—but memories of empty chairs, missed birthdays, and long silences echoed louder than his words.

"I'm not sure I can," she said, her voice barely above a whisper. "I've worked so hard to become someone I like. Someone I trust. I can't risk undoing that."

"I'm not here to take anything away," he said. "Just to be part of whatever life you've built. Even if it's just a small corner."

They sat in silence for a while. Finally, Haylee looked up. "Maybe we start slow," she said. "You can see what this life looks like—for me. And we figure it out from there."

His shoulders dropped, a quiet relief settling over him. "That's more than I hoped for."

In the days that followed, they found a rhythm—simple routines, shared meals, short hikes with Josie. Her father didn't push. He listened more than he talked. He was trying. And Haylee, guarded as she was, began to let small pieces of her wall down.

But she never stopped being careful. Healing wasn't instant. It was slow, layered, and fragile.

One afternoon, after a hike through the nearby woods, they returned to Bertha, laughing over an old story he'd told about her as a toddler. The laughter faded when Haylee checked her phone.

129

Another text.

Unknown Number: *"You shouldn't have let him in. Some things are better left buried."*

Her breath caught. Her fingers hovered over the screen. The camp's sounds—distant laughter, the occasional crackle from someone's firepit—blurred in the background. The message was sharper this time. Less cryptic, more threatening.

She quickly turned off her phone, her hand trembling slightly. This wasn't just someone being dramatic. This was someone watching.

She glanced at her father, who was unzipping his jacket, oblivious. For a moment, she almost told him. But something stopped her. He'd only just gotten here. If she dropped this on him now, it might undo whatever fragile progress they'd made.

That night, sleep didn't come easy. She lay in her bunk, listening to the soft, rhythmic breathing of her dog curled beside her. The glow of the moon filtered through the window blinds, casting pale shadows on the ceiling. The message replayed in her head, again and again.

Some things are better left buried.

Was it about her aunt? About her mother? Was someone watching her movements—waiting for her to dig too deep?

Haylee thought back to the journal entries. The pages her aunt had written. Some of them had hinted at secrets—unfinished thoughts, names she didn't recognize, places she had never been. Could they be connected?

She didn't know who was sending them. But this one felt different. More pointed. More dangerous.

She forced a smile as she tucked the phone away.

"Everything okay?" her father asked.

"Yeah," she said, reaching for the kettle. "Just tired. Let's make some tea."

But her mind was elsewhere.

Because someone out there wasn't just watching.

They knew something.

And they were getting closer.

She stared into the dark until her eyes blurred, her thoughts tangled in uncertainty. There was so much she didn't know. About her family. About the things they'd never said aloud. And now, it seemed, someone else knew more than she did.

The past had found its way back to her doorstep. And this time, it wasn't just looking for closure. It was warning her.

And Haylee had no idea what it might cost to find the truth.

Ending of a long day

That night, long after her father had fallen asleep on the foldout bed, Haylee sat upright in her own bunk, wrapped in a blanket, staring at the faint glow of her phone screen. She'd turned it to silent, checked the lock screen too many times. No new messages. But the damage had already been done. The words from the unknown number clung to her like a fog, curling around her thoughts with icy fingers. You shouldn't have let him in. She wanted to believe it was just someone playing games. But something about it felt calculated. Personal.

Outside, the wind stirred the pine trees, their branches brushing against the RV's roof in slow, scratching arcs. Josie lifted her head once, ears twitching, then settled again. Even she seemed on edge. Haylee glanced over at her father, sleeping soundly, unaware. There was something almost cruel about that—that he could sleep so easily while her own mind was a tangle of memories, questions, and now, fear.

The next morning, Haylee woke from a restless sleep with a pounding headache and a hollow pit in her stomach. She forced herself to smile as she poured coffee, trying not to let the exhaustion show. Her father, noticing the bags under her eyes, asked gently, "You okay?" She nodded. "Didn't sleep great. That's all." But the lie sat heavy on her tongue. She didn't tell him about the text. She wasn't ready. Not yet.

Over the next few days, she tried to shake the feeling—telling herself she was just being paranoid. She stayed busy: hikes with Josie, journaling at the riverbank, errands into town. But the sense of being watched never fully left. Sometimes, when she glanced up from her writing, she swore she saw a shape in the distance that disappeared too quickly. A truck that drove by too slowly. A face in a crowd she couldn't quite place. And always, there was the journal—her aunt's words calling her deeper into questions she hadn't been ready to ask.

Chapter 22:
Stepping Into the Unknown

The days were slipping by quickly now. It had been a couple of weeks since her father arrived, and though their relationship was still in its early stages of repair, Haylee felt a cautious optimism building inside her. They had shared more meals together, more stories, and a few quiet moments that had allowed her to see her father not just as the man who had detached from her when her mother died, but as a human being capable of growth. That alone was a small victory.

But Haylee was still walking a tightrope. There was a part of her that wasn't sure if she could ever truly forgive him for all the years of silence, the years of missed birthdays and holidays. It was hard to forget how much she had learned to do on her own, how much of herself she had built without him.

Still, it felt like she was on the cusp of something new, and that feeling—the one that had guided her across the country, the one that had sparked her desire to start over—was pulling at her again. It was calling her to embrace the unknown, to lean into the changes happening in her life, no matter how messy they felt.

One thing had become clear: she was not the same person she had been when she first left her old life behind. And she wasn't going back. But something her father said chimed in the back of her mind. He had something he needed to talk to her about. In all of the bonding, she had forgotten about it until that last text message came in. She didn't know what to think.

Things were getting better between them. She thought it was best for him to bring it up rather than poke the bear.

It was a sunny afternoon, and Haylee and her dad had taken a drive out to a nearby town. They had found a quaint little farmers' market, and as they wandered through the rows of fresh produce and homemade crafts, Haylee couldn't help but feel the familiar tug of nostalgia.

It reminded her of when she and her aunt used to travel to small towns together, exploring the local markets, trying new foods, and laughing at the eccentricities of the people they met along the way.

Her dad could see the faraway look in her eyes, but he didn't say anything at first. He had learned over the past few weeks that Haylee wasn't someone who needed to be fixed—she just needed space to process.

"I'm glad you came with me today," Haylee said, breaking the silence. She turned to him, her expression soft but thoughtful. "It's been good to get out of the RV park for a bit."

"I think it's good for both of us. I mean, when was the last time we actually did something like this?"

She chuckled, brushing a strand of hair from her face. "It's been too long. I guess I've been focused on… well, everything else."

The two of them continued wandering through the market, sampling fruits and homemade pies, chatting with the vendors, and soaking in the easygoing atmosphere of small-town life. It felt good to be in this moment, away from the complexities of the past few weeks. For the first time in a long time, Haylee felt a sense of peace, as though she were exactly where she was supposed to be.

But as they turned a corner, Haylee spotted something that brought her to a sudden halt: an old wooden sign, weathered by years of wind and rain. It was a small antique shop, the kind that seemed to have been frozen in time. She felt a surge of emotion rise within her, as if the place had somehow called her.

"Do you mind if we check it out?" she asked her dad, her voice quiet, almost reverent.

"Of course," he replied, his eyes following hers. "Let's go see what treasures they have in there."

They stepped inside the dimly lit shop, the musty scent of old wood and vintage trinkets surrounding them. It was exactly what Haylee had expected: shelves filled with oddities, faded photographs, old furniture, and dusty knick-knacks from bygone eras. It was like stepping into another world—a world of memories and forgotten stories.

As she wandered deeper into the shop, something caught her eye. In a corner, on a small, cluttered table, was an old, leather-bound journal. It wasn't particularly remarkable at first glance—just another piece of antique clutter. But when Haylee reached for it, she felt an odd connection to it, as if something about it called to her.

She flipped it open to the first page, her fingers grazing the brittle paper. The handwriting inside was elegant, delicate, and familiar.

"To my dear Haylee, may this guide you when you need it most."

Her heart skipped a beat. It was her aunt's handwriting.

"Dad…" Haylee whispered, her voice trembling with disbelief. She turned the journal around, showing him the inscription.

He looked at her, his brow furrowed. "Your aunt's? But… what is this doing here?"

"I don't know." Haylee could barely believe what she was holding.

Her mind raced as she flipped through the journal's pages. There were notes, lists, sketches of places she and her aunt had visited, and even little anecdotes from their time together. It was a part of her aunt's world that Haylee had never seen before.

"This was meant for me," Haylee whispered to herself. She could feel the weight of it in her hands, the connection to her aunt stronger than ever.

For a moment, she just stood there, absorbing the significance of the find. Her aunt had left this for her, just as she had left so many other things—the postcards, the truck, the RV. But this was different. This was something intimate. Something that only Haylee could understand.

Her dad was quiet for a moment, then stepped closer, resting his hand gently on her shoulder. "You okay?" he asked softly.

Haylee nodded, her eyes still fixed on the pages. "I think I've been searching for answers in all the wrong places. Maybe this is what I was supposed to find."

Back at the RV park, that night, Haylee sat in the dim light of the lantern, the journal open in her lap. The pages seemed to whisper secrets, as though her aunt were still there, guiding her through the journey she had started so many months ago.

Her dad had gone to bed early, but Haylee couldn't sleep. There was too much on her mind. She flipped through the journal, each page a window into her aunt's life, and yet each page was a mirror reflecting her own journey. The drawings, the travel notes, the musings on the open road—it was as if her aunt had been living the same kind of life Haylee was now leading. She hadn't just left her a physical space in the RV park; her aunt had left behind a piece of her spirit, waiting for Haylee to discover it.

There was a passage near the end of the journal that stood out to Haylee:

"To live fully, to live freely, is not to run from the past, but to honor it, learn from it, and then let it go. Only then can you truly live for yourself. Find your peace, Haylee. Find your way."

Tears pricked at Haylee's eyes as she read the words, each syllable resonating deep inside her. Her aunt had known. She had understood that Haylee needed to let go of the guilt, the anger, the confusion of the past, in order to step forward into her own future.

Haylee sat there for a long time, the journal cradled in her hands. The fire of the campfire flickered outside, casting soft shadows on the walls of Bertha. And for the first time in a long time, Haylee felt something shift inside her—a quiet understanding, a peace that had eluded her for years.

She wasn't running anymore. She wasn't afraid of what lay ahead. She was exactly where she needed to be.

Chapter 23:
Embracing the Future

The morning light filtered through the trees, casting long shadows over the RV park. Haylee sat on the small porch of Bertha, a cup of coffee cradled in her hands, her aunt's journal resting beside her. She had stayed up late the night before, poring over the final entries, each one a quiet revelation. The words felt less like memories and more like a map—guiding her toward something she hadn't even known she was looking for.

For years, she'd been running. From the grief. From the silence. From the pain of a life that hadn't gone as planned. But as the steam rose from her mug and the sun touched the tops of the trees, Haylee realized she didn't have to run anymore. Her aunt's voice lived in those pages with gentle wisdom, reminding her that living fully wasn't about escaping the past—it was about facing it, learning from it, and choosing to move forward anyway.

It was a lesson she finally felt ready to accept.

As the day wore on, Haylee moved through her routine with a lighter spirit. She wiped the dust from Bertha, adjusted a latch that had come loose, and shared lunch with her father. There was a steadiness to her movements now, a quiet confidence she hadn't known she possessed. She no longer felt the need to prove herself—to anyone. She had let go of the guilt, the old expectations, and the fear. In their place, she had found something that felt suspiciously like peace.

That afternoon, she found her father outside, adjusting the small solar panel he'd recently bought.

"You know," he said, glancing up, "I've been thinking... Maybe it's time to really take Bertha out. Go see some of those places your aunt wrote about. Not just sit here talking about it—actually do it."

Haylee's heart gave a small leap. It was exactly what she needed, even if she hadn't said it out loud. The idea of retracing her aunt's footsteps, of exploring those places through her own lens, felt right—like the next chapter was finally ready to be written.

"That sounds amazing," she said with a smile. "I think it's time."

The following week, they packed up—maps, food, extra gear—and said their goodbyes to the RV park. Her father, now a steady presence in her life, offered help with the route and Bertha's maintenance. But Haylee took the lead. She needed to. This journey had always been hers.

The open road stretched ahead like a blank page. With Josie curled on the couch and Bella peeking from the dashboard, Haylee drove into a future still undefined—but completely hers.

They stopped in quiet towns, wandered through forests, and waded in still lakes. Each place felt like a new piece of her story. Conversations with her father flowed more easily now—sometimes filled with laughter, other times heavy with truth. But always, they were real. And for the first time, she felt like she truly saw him—not just the father she'd wanted, but the man who was trying to be better.

One evening, they camped by a serene lake. The stars came out slowly, casting reflections across the water. Haylee sat by the fire, fingering the crystal ring her aunt had given her. It glinted in the firelight like a silent promise.

"This is perfect," she murmured.

Her father looked at her, his voice soft. "It's been a long journey, hasn't it?"

Then, more hesitantly, he added, "I think we both needed this."

Before she could answer, her phone buzzed again. Another message from the unknown number. Her heart stilled, and this time her dad noticed.

"What's the matter?" he asked, his tone instantly serious.

Haylee hesitated, then slowly handed him the phone. "I've been getting these texts. I don't know who's sending them... but they're warning me about someone."

He looked at the screen, his brow furrowing.

"There's something I need to tell you," he said, his voice tight. "It's part of the reason I came to find you."

Her stomach turned. "Okay," she whispered.

"I know things have gotten better between us. And I don't want this to change that." He paused, clearly struggling. "You know how Agnes was always in your life… how she'd take you for the summers?"

Haylee nodded, wary. "Yeah…"

He swallowed hard, staring at his hands. "It was a different time. Your mother and I… we couldn't have children. When we found out Agnes was pregnant… we thought it was a blessing."

Haylee stared at him, eyes narrowing. "What are you saying?"

He pulled an envelope from the back of a photo album. Inside was a worn hospital photo—Aggie in a bed, holding a newborn. Haylee.

"I—I don't understand."

"She didn't give you up because she didn't love you," he said quickly. "She wanted you to have a stable life. But she never left you. She was always around. She loved you more than anything."

Haylee stood abruptly, the photo clutched in her hand. "So, my whole life has been a lie."

"No," he said gently. "It was love. Complicated, messy love. But never a lie."

She stormed off, Josie close behind, pacing the perimeter of their firelight. Tears blurred her vision. She wanted to scream, to disappear into the night.

Eventually, she returned. Her father sat quietly, waiting. She dropped into the chair beside him, silent.

He didn't reach for her, just said, "I don't expect you to understand tonight. I just thought… you should know."

Haylee's voice cracked. "I want to know everything. Just… not right now. I need time."

He nodded. "When you're ready."

They sat in silence, the fire crackling between them. Haylee stared into the flames, her heart too full to speak. That night, sleep came in fragments. But when it did, Aggie was there—in a dream, arms open, smiling with relief.

The next morning, Haylee awoke with a strange sense of calm. Something had shifted. The truth hadn't broken her—it had peeled back a layer, revealed something raw and real underneath.

As they packed up camp and climbed back into Bertha, her father handed her a cup of coffee. "I know I dropped a lot on you," he said. "But I'm proud of you, Haylee. I always have been."

She looked at him then, truly looked. Not just as the man who raised her, but the man who had carried secrets, regrets, and now, courage.

"I'm still processing," she said softly. "But I'm glad you're here."

They drove in silence for a while, the road stretching ahead. For the first time, Haylee didn't feel lost.

With Josie and Bella by her side, and the truth behind her—raw, imperfect, and real—Haylee knew one thing with certainty:

This was just the beginning.

Letting the Air Out

The road unfurled before them like an unwritten page, and Haylee let the hum of Bertha's engine soothe the turmoil still swirling in her chest. Her father sat quietly beside her, sensing the fragility of the air between them. Neither of them spoke for miles, but it wasn't uncomfortable—it was just... tender. The truth had been spoken, and now they were suspended in the quiet aftermath, each of them trying to find footing on the new ground they'd uncovered.

As the landscape shifted from forest to wide open fields, Haylee glanced out at the horizon. For the first time, she wasn't sure how to define herself. Daughter? Niece? Both? Neither? It felt like she was caught between two versions of her own story— and somehow, both were true. The ache in her chest wasn't just about the truth itself, but about the years lost to silence, to secrets. And yet, beneath that ache, something steadier was taking root: clarity.

That evening, they stopped near a state park with a view of the mountains. While her father worked on lighting a fire, Haylee took Josie for a walk along a quiet trail. The sun dipped low behind the trees, casting golden light over the leaves. She pressed a hand to her chest, right over the crystal ring, and closed her eyes. "You knew," she whispered. "And you still stayed close. Thank you."

Back at camp, she found her father setting two mugs of tea on the makeshift table. "I wasn't sure if you were up for talking tonight," he said gently. "But I made tea, just in case."

Haylee sat down beside him and accepted the tea. "Thank you," she said, her voice soft but steadier than she expected. "For telling me. For not letting it stay a secret forever."

He looked relieved. "I've thought about it every day. How to tell you. When. And what it would mean."

"It changes a lot," she admitted. "But it also... explains some things. Like why I always felt a little different. Why did Aggie and I have that bond? I thought it was just a coincidence. But it wasn't."

"No, it wasn't," he said. "She never stopped loving you. None of us did."

They sipped their tea in silence, watching the fire crackle between them. For the first time, Haylee felt that she could breathe around the truth. It still hurt—it probably always would—but the pain had edges now. It wasn't the shapeless confusion she'd lived with for so long. It was something she could examine, learn from, maybe even grow around.

Unraveling Secrets

Later that night, she lay in her bunk and opened the journal again, her fingers brushing over Aggie's looping handwriting. A sentence caught her eye—one she must have read before, but hadn't felt until now: "The truth has a strange way of setting us free, but only after it breaks us open."

Tears slid silently down her cheeks, but this time, they weren't from confusion or anger. They were released.

The next morning, the world felt different. Lighter. Her father handed her a fresh cup of coffee with a smile that, for once, wasn't cautious or uncertain. It was warm, real, and familiar. She took it with a nod of gratitude and leaned against the side of Bertha, watching the steam rise in the early light.

They didn't need to talk much that morning. Instead, they packed up camp with a quiet rhythm, falling into a shared cadence that didn't need explanation. It felt like a partnership now—tentative, healing, and new.

As they pulled onto the highway, Haylee glanced at her father and then at the horizon stretching out ahead. There were still questions, still unknowns, and probably more pain to come. But there was also a road—and that meant forward.

And forward was enough.

As they cruised down a dusty back road later that afternoon, Haylee's phone buzzed again on the dashboard. She picked it up warily. Another message. Same number. This time, the words were different:

"You don't know the whole story. Aggie was protecting more than just you."

Her heart thudded in her chest as she read it aloud. Her father's brows furrowed, his grip tightening on the steering wheel.

"That's not just someone playing games," he said. "That's someone who knows something."

They pulled over at a gas station, tension simmering between them. Haylee quickly scrolled back through the old texts—each one more cryptic than the last. Her father leaned over her shoulder, scanning the screen. "I don't like this," he muttered. "And if they're right—if Agnes was hiding something else—we need to figure out what."

Haylee nodded, her mind racing. "Do you think it's about my birth? Or something else?"

"I don't know," he said, shaking his head. "But your aunt was always more involved in things than she let on. She kept journals. Letters. Maybe there's more we haven't found yet."

That night, back at camp, they sat across from one another under a lantern's soft glow, digging through the boxes of Aggie's things they had packed along for the journey. Old letters. Unfinished postcards. A half-sealed envelope with a name Haylee didn't recognize.

As the firelight danced over the pages, Haylee realized something: her aunt's past wasn't fully buried. And whatever secrets she'd taken to the grave were starting to surface.

Chapter 24:
Shadows in the Ink

The road stretched out in front of them, a ribbon of asphalt winding through tall pines and rolling hills, but Haylee's thoughts weren't on the scenery. They were on the journal tucked away in her bag—the one that had once offered comfort and clarity, but now pulsed with unanswered questions.

They had driven in silence for over an hour, her father respecting the space she clearly needed. But as the miles passed, Haylee's curiosity gnawed at her. Something about the mysterious text messages and last night's revelation had unsettled her. Why now? Why these warnings? And why did the journal suddenly feel… incomplete?

At their next stop—a quiet, remote turnout overlooking a sun-drenched valley— Haylee finally pulled the journal into her lap. She flipped through its pages, familiar with most of them by heart. But now, she was looking not for comfort, but for clues.

"Dad," she said slowly, "do you remember if Aggie ever talked about someone she trusted with... secrets? I mean, something beyond the stories she told or the things she wrote?"

Her father, setting down the travel mug in his hands, furrowed his brow. "Not specifically. She was private, sure, but she had her way of telling the truth without ever fully telling it. Why?"

Haylee ran her fingers across the pages. "I think there's something hidden here. I'm not sure how or why, but these entries—some of them read like they're speaking in code. Like she was trying to say something without coming right out and saying it. And there is something about Bertha. I see things, smell things, and then there's this trunk under the bed." She revealed.

Her father leaned over, looking at the open journal. "What are you saying?"

Her father's brow furrowed, concern flickering in his eyes. "What kind of things?"

Haylee hesitated. "Sometimes it's just a scent—lavender and smoke, all at once. And sometimes... it's more. Shadows that move where they shouldn't. Whispers that come through the vents, but they're not in any language I know. And then there's the texts."

He went still.

Last night, one of the messages said, 'It watches from where she left it. Aggie never sealed it properly.'"

Her father sat down heavily, his face pale. "That trunk belonged to my mother."

Haylee looked at him, heart racing. "Then maybe Aggie wasn't crazy like everyone thought. Maybe she was trying to contain it. And now it's waiting for someone else to open it."

There was a silence between them, thick and heavy. Then Haylee added in a whisper, "And I think it wants me to."

"I think Aggie knew something," Haylee said. "Something she was afraid to put in plain words. And I think these texts... maybe they're connected to that."

They sat there for a moment, the sound of birdsong and the distant whisper of wind filling the space between them. What had begun as a personal journey was becoming something more. The past wasn't finished with Haylee yet—and the road ahead held more than healing.

It held answers.

Shift in the Air

The journal lay open on the small dinette table inside Bertha, the late afternoon light casting golden stripes across the pages. Haylee sat across from her dad, a notebook and pen in hand, while he gently turned the fragile pages of Aggie's worn leather journal. Josie rested on the floor at their feet, her ears twitching occasionally as if she, too, was paying attention.

The night before still echoed in Haylee's chest like the final notes of a song she wasn't ready to stop listening to. The truth of her origin had cracked something deep inside her—shocked her, reshaped her. But it hadn't broken her. If anything, it had made her more curious. More determined.

"What if the texts are connected to this?" she asked, her voice hushed, almost reverent. "To all the things she never said out loud—but maybe wrote down?"

Her dad nodded slowly. "That's what I've been wondering too. When I said there was something I needed to tell you... well, it wasn't just the truth about Aggie being your mother. It was about what happened before she passed. She told me she was afraid. Said someone had been asking questions—about her past.

About you."
Haylee's pen stilled on the page. "Why didn't you say something sooner?"

He sighed. "Because I didn't know what it meant. And because I was scared. I thought maybe it was just Agnes being Agnes—always protective, always a little mysterious. But now... with those messages you're getting... I think we should take them seriously."

Haylee flipped back through the journal, eyes scanning for anything that might hint at secrets. There were plenty of heartfelt entries, travel sketches, and snippets of poetry. But every so often, there were passages that felt... different. Like Aggie had deliberately been vague. References to "him," or to "a choice I had no right to make." Sentences scribbled out, or single lines that ended mid-thought.

Her dad leaned in. "She told me once that some truths weren't meant to be told all at once.

That she kept pieces of her life in different places—journals, letters, even cassette tapes. She said if anything ever happened to her, the ones who needed to know would find them. If they paid attention."

Haylee's heart thudded. "Then we start here. We found those pieces."

He smiled faintly. "You really are her daughter, you know."

She let out a small laugh, though her nerves buzzed. "Guess we're about to find out what else Aggie was keeping hidden."

As the sun dipped toward the horizon, they began marking sections of the journal, pulling out recurring names, places, and dates. One name kept appearing in different forms—initials, a last name scribbled in the margin, always near mentions of "consequences" or "that summer." The more they looked, the more it felt like Aggie had left a trail. Not to confuse, but to guide. As if she knew Haylee might one day need to follow it.

And now, that day has come.

What's in a Name?

The next morning, after a quiet breakfast by the lake, Haylee and her dad sat down with the journal spread open between them. They had spent the evening before marking passages that seemed significant, but now it was time to connect the dots.

"Look at this," Haylee said, pointing to a series of entries dated around the same time. "Aggie mentions a 'meeting in the woods,' but there's no context. No names, just 'the usual place.'"

Her dad leaned in, squinting at the faded ink. "That could be anything. A group of friends, a secret club..."

"Or something more," Haylee interrupted. "What if this 'meeting' was something she didn't want anyone to know about? Something she thought was too dangerous to write plainly?"

Haylee frowned. "There's more. In the journal, she mentioned a cabin. She called it the place of forgetting. She wrote about going there for meetings—only she never said who with. Just… 'Elliot.'"

At the mention of the name, her dad stiffened. "Elliot? That's not a name I've heard in a long time."

"You knew him?"

He hesitated. "I knew *of* him. Elliot was... around, when Agnes was younger. Some said he was just a family friend. Others said he was more than that—into things Aggie never spoke about in daylight. people used to whisper they met out in the woods, in the old cabin that belonged to her. After a while, folks stopped asking. Aggie didn't answer certain questions."

Haylee turned the page in the journal, voice barely above a whisper. "She wrote, *Elliot says the veil is thinning. We must reinforce the seal before the equinox. If Haylee ever finds this, I pray it's not too late.*"

149

Her father looked at her then, not with confusion—but with recognition. "Aggie never believed in coincidence," he said. "If she left that message, it was meant for you." He stood and walked toward the trunk, stopping only to add, "And if Elliot's name is showing up again, it means something's stirring. Something she tried to keep buried."

Haylee glanced at the trunk too. The air around it felt heavier now, as if the room itself was holding its breath.

And deep inside, something was beginning to wake up.

He nodded thoughtfully. "It's possible. Agnes was always careful with her words. If she was involved in something... unsavory, she might have hidden it in plain sight."

They spent the next few hours cross-referencing the journal entries with the map they'd been using for their travels. They marked locations Aggie had visited, places she had written about, and any mention of names or events that seemed out of place.

Haylee took everything out of the trunk and reexamined it over and over. Hoping she missed something the first or fifth time.

One name kept recurring: "Elliot." Sometimes just the first name, sometimes a full name with no last name. It was always associated with vague phrases like "the deal," "the arrangement," and "the price."

"Who is Elliot?" Haylee wondered aloud. "And what kind of deal was Aggie involved in?"

Her dad rubbed his temples. "I don't know. But I think we're getting closer to understanding what happened."

Down the Rabbit Hole

They decided to follow the trail. The next entry in the journal mentioned a small town in the mountains—a place Aggie had visited frequently. It was a long shot, but it was the only lead they had.

Packing up Bertha, they set off toward the mountains, with Josie and Bella nestled in the back. The drive was scenic but uneventful, and as they approached the town, Haylee felt a mix of anticipation and dread.

They stopped at a local diner to ask around. The waitress, an older woman with sharp eyes, seemed to recognize Aggie's name and picture immediately.

"Aggie?" she said, her voice tinged with suspicion. "She used to come through here a lot. Always with that man. Quiet fellow. Never said much."

"Do you know his name?" Haylee asked, leaning forward.

The waitress hesitated, then shook her head. "I never asked. Didn't seem right. But they were always together. Always."

"Did they ever talk about anything? Anything unusual?" her dad pressed.

The waitress thought for a moment. "Well, now that you mention it, they did talk about a place. A cabin up in the hills. Said it was 'the safest place.'"

Haylee's heart raced. "Do you know where this cabin is?"

She nodded slowly. "I think so. But it's been years. You'd have to ask someone else."

Thanking her, they left the diner and headed to the local library. There, they found an old map of the area and pinpointed the location of the cabin. It was deep in the woods, far from any main roads.

With the map in hand, they set out toward the cabin, the air growing cooler as they ascended into the mountains.

The journey was challenging, the path overgrown and winding, but they pressed on.

As they reached the clearing where the cabin stood, Haylee felt a chill run down her spine. It sat hunched beneath a canopy of pines miles out from town, barely visible from the road, as if the woods were trying to reclaim it. The structure was weathered and abandoned. Weathered boards and a moss-covered roof made it look abandoned, but when Haylee stepped onto the porch, the hairs on her arms rose.

There was something unsettling about it. The windows were boarded up, and the door hung ajar, creaking in the wind.

"She came here a lot?" she asked.

Her father nodded, unlocking the door with a rusted key. "Every full moon. For decades. She said it was for solitude. But Aggie never did anything without pur pose."

The air inside was thick with the scent of dried herbs and something older—earthy, metallic. Not rot exactly, but close.

Haylee wandered in slowly, her eyes falling on the dust-covered table near the hearth. Scratched into its surface, mostly hidden by a stack of old books, was a symbol she'd never seen before: a circle intersected by three lines, one broken. Josie and Bella stayed close.

In the corner, Haylee spotted something—a small, leather-bound notebook.

When she brushed her fingers across it, the air shifted. Just a little. Like the cabin had inhaled.

.She picked it up, brushing off the dust. It was Aggie's handwriting.

Opening the first page, she read aloud, *"If you're reading this, then I've gone too far. Elliot is not who he seems. The deal was never meant to be kept. The truth is buried here."*

Her dad took the notebook from her, scanning the pages. "This is it," he said quietly. "The final piece."

They had found Aggie's last message. But what did it mean? And what was the truth she had buried?

Chapter 25:
The Path Less Travelled

The early morning sun cast a golden hue across the desert landscape, stretching out like a welcome mat to the day ahead. Haylee stood outside Bertha, her gaze fixed on the wide open spaces before her. The road stretched endlessly, but for the first time in a long while, she didn't feel intimidated by the unknown. Instead, she felt a quiet anticipation—like standing on the edge of a cliff, ready to leap into something entirely new.

Behind her, her father was quietly packing up the remnants of last night's campfire. His movements were calm and methodical, a contrast to the emotional whirlwind they'd weathered in recent days. Now, though, there was something steadier in the air between them—something healing.

The road had done something to her. Its stillness, its vast, unspoken wisdom had given her space to think—to breathe. For the first time, she had been able to hear her own thoughts without them being drowned out by noise or fear.

"Thank you," she said softly.

Her dad looked up, the morning light catching in his eyes. She continued, "I know it wasn't easy to tell me about Aggie. About... everything. I want you to know, I'm not angry anymore. I had a good life. A happy one. The details don't change that."

There was a long pause, filled with quiet understanding. He didn't speak, just nodded and held her gaze. She reached out and took his hand.

"Is there anything else I should know? In light of... everything?"

His answer was simple. "No."

That word, and the certainty behind it, gave her peace.

As they finished packing, Haylee slipped the black tourmaline ring off the chain around her neck and held it in her palm.

Add a little bit of boIt had started as a gift from Aggie, but it had become so much more—a tether to her roots, and a symbol of the strength she'd found along the way. She slid it onto her left index finger, and for the first time, it felt like it belonged there. A quiet hope bloomed in her chest.

"Let's go," she said, patting Josie's side before climbing into the RV. "Time to hit the road."

Her father didn't say anything else that night, but Haylee could tell he knew more than he was letting on. The name *Elliot* lingered between them like smoke that wouldn't clear.

Later, after her dad had gone to bed, she found herself staring at the trunk again. The whispering had stopped—but only after she touched it. That was the part that bothered her most. Tucked in the corner of the truck was a faded photograph.

Haylee picked it up carefully. The image showed Aggie, younger, standing beside a man with sharp eyes and a crooked smile. His hand was on her shoulder. On the back, in Aggie's handwriting: *Elliot – between.*

"Between what?" Haylee whispered.

Her father looked at the picture over her shoulder. "That's the part no one could explain." Haylee jumped at his voice. "Some said he was a medium. Others said he wasn't even human. Just something pretending to be."

Haylee turned back to the symbol on the trunk. Without meaning to, she traced it again. This time, something flickered inside. A cold flash of light—then gone.

She gasped. "Did you see that?"

He looked, but it was already still again. "What happened?"

"I don't know. I felt… pulled, for a second. Like it recognized me."

Her father finally met her eyes.

"There's more to you than you've been told, Haylee. Your mother—Agnes—she didn't just keep secrets. She carried a legacy. One that doesn't end with her."

Haylee stared at the photo again. She could feel something just beneath the surface, like the ground before an earthquake. A memory that didn't belong to her.

And then she heard it—just a whisper. In the space between her heartbeat.

The blood remembers.

The next few days passed in a blur of dusty highways, roadside stops, and wide-open skies. They wandered through quaint towns and hidden hiking trails, discovering small joys tucked into every mile. At each stop, Haylee felt a little more grounded in herself. She wasn't searching anymore—she was living.

One evening, they pulled into a small campground on the edge of a sleepy town called Silverton. Haylee was tired but buzzing with quiet excitement. After setting up for the night, they joined a handful of other travelers around a communal fire. The stars blinked to life above them as strangers swapped stories, sharing memories and laughter like old friends.

There were retired couples chasing one last adventure, young drifters with guitars and dreams, solo travelers like her. As Haylee listened, a deep warmth spread through her. These people—they were part of something bigger. And now, so was she.

Later, long after the fire burned low and others had gone to bed, she stayed out, gazing up at the stars. Her dad had turned in early—he was catching a flight out of Silverton the next morning. There were things he needed to follow up on, old friends he thought might have answers about Aggie's past. Still, it felt strange to see him go.

Before heading to bed, he called back to her over his shoulder.

"Hey, Haylee? I'm really proud of you, you know. You've come a long way."

The words caught her off guard—simple, but full of meaning. Her chest ached in that good way, where love sits deep.

"Thanks, Dad," she said softly. It wasn't everything, but it was a start.

The next morning, as they packed up their site, her dad turned to her with a sheepish look.

"I'm going to miss you," he admitted.

"I'll miss you too."

He smiled and added, "You know... you can always come visit. Maybe even stay a while. Write. Do your thing."

She froze. Writing. It had been so long since she'd thought of herself that way—as a storyteller. Her focus had been survival, self-discovery. But the road had changed something in her.

"You think I'm ready for that?" she asked.

He didn't hesitate. "I think you've been ready for a long time. You just needed space to remember who you are."

The words rooted in her, settling deep.

"Maybe you're right," she whispered, feeling something stir—something that felt like purpose.

As they drove toward the tiny Silverton airport, the dusty skyline rising in the distance, Haylee reflected on how far she'd come. She'd left behind a version of herself that lived in fear, tangled in uncertainty.

And now, she was something new: someone unafraid to step into the unknown. Someone who could write her own next chapter.

She didn't have all the answers—not yet. But she had the road, the sky, the hum of possibility.

And for now, that was more than enough.

Chapter 26:
Words and Roads

This trip with her dad had been an eye-opener, to say the least. Not just because of the bombshell revelation that Aggie was actually her mom, but because of what it took internally for Haylee to fully understand that truth. It was maturity—the kind you can't fake or force—that allowed her to see the past through a different lens.

For the first time, she truly thought about how hard it must have been for Aggie to let her go. She hadn't walked away because she didn't care. In fact, it was the opposite. Aggie had chosen to give Haylee the gift of a stable family—one with two loving parents who could raise her in a way Aggie, at the time, couldn't. That sacrifice wasn't abandonment. It was selflessness, pure and quiet.

Haylee had never really asked why she was an only child. She hadn't needed more. Her parents had given her everything she could have wanted: love, attention, consistency. And then there were the summers with Aggie—"Aunt Aggie," as she had always known her—those memory-drenched days filled with wild freedom and laughter. Aggie let her eat cake for dinner, ride in the back of pickup trucks, and stay up watching movies well past midnight. It wasn't reckless; it was just... looser. Easier. Her parents enforced the rules: vegetables, sunscreen, helmets. Aggie offered moments that made her feel alive.

It was those little things that made summer with Aggie feel so sacred. Looking back now, Haylee understood what Aggie had given her, both as an aunt and as a mother. Freedom, with a safety net of love.

She said a heartfelt goodbye to her dad that afternoon. They'd promised to stay in closer touch, and for the first time, Haylee truly believed they would. As she walked back to Bertha and the girls, she felt something settle in her chest. A sense of home. Not a house or a destination—but home, in the truest sense. She wasn't racing toward deadlines or pushing herself to be anyone but who she was. This journey wasn't measured in miles anymore—it was measured in growth.

She was unfolding on her own terms. Just like she had during those childhood summers, Haylee felt free again.

Through Softer Eyes

By the end of the week, she had filled ten full pages in her journal—more than she had ever written in her life. Each page was a window into her soul, a breadcrumb on the path of self-discovery. It had become unexpectedly therapeutic, a kind of mirror she hadn't known she needed.

One warm afternoon, journal tucked under her arm, she wandered down to the lake. The water shimmered in the sunlight, and there, sitting on the bank, was Josie. She was crouched close to the edge, her eyes wide as she watched fish leap through the surface.

When Haylee approached, Josie looked up.

"Can I get in the water?" she asked.

Haylee smiled. "Yeah, go ahead."

Josie plunged in with delight, sending up glittering sprays of water as she splashed and played, arms flailing in an attempt to catch a fish. There was a moment Haylee thought she might actually succeed—and a moment of relief when she didn't. From the edge of the bank, Haylee laughed, light and full. Bella meandered over, curious, but retreated quickly when a stray splash hit her fur. She turned and trotted back to Bertha in search of dry, cozy refuge.

In the simplicity of that moment, Haylee realized how much the girls had taught her. Josie, with her fearless joy and uninhibited spirit. Bella, with her lazy grace and preference for calm. Together, they were showing Haylee a different way to see the world—a way that had nothing to do with control and everything to do with presence. With each day, Haylee was learning to look at life with softer eyes.

That night, after washing the lake water from Josie's hair and tucking her into bed, Haylee felt it—a sense of closure. Not an ending, but the start of something deeper. This time in the park had been a reset, the first true step of a longer journey. She wasn't just letting go of her old life anymore. She was stepping fully into the new one.

That same night, she opened YouTube for the first time since her dad's visit and recorded a video. It wasn't polished. It wasn't even planned. But it was honest. Raw. She spoke about how each stretch of road had taught her something new—not just about the world, but about herself. She spoke about Aggie, about freedom, about reflection. About Josie, Bella, and the little moments that were shaping her not into someone new, but into someone more whole.

The comments and likes poured in faster than she expected. Messages from people who had started their own travels for different reasons—a remote job, a cross-country move, a post-retirement dream—but all of them echoing the same realization: being in the moment was everything. The simplicity of now had more value than anything they'd left behind.

The next morning, Haylee packed up Bertha and made her way down the mountain road. The park had given her clarity, but the road still called. She knew she couldn't stay in that peaceful bubble forever. Life moved, and now, so would she.

But this time, she wasn't afraid of what was next.

Writer's Circle

As the trees blurred past her windows, Haylee smiled, thinking about how much had changed. Her relationship with her dad had deepened. Her sense of identity had expanded. She was no longer just a traveler trying to find herself—she was a woman learning how to be herself.

She glanced over at the girls, Josie sprawled across the bench with a stuffed raccoon in her arms, Bella curled at her feet like a shadow.

"Next stop, where to?" she asked aloud, knowing neither of them would answer—but feeling, for the first time, that she didn't need one.

Haylee smiled. And drove.

The road curved gently as the trees began to thin, replaced by wide, open skies and golden fields that shimmered in the late morning light. Haylee rolled the window down, letting the breeze wash over her. Josie was dreaming quietly in the back, while Bella let out a satisfied meow from her corner, her ears flopping lazily with each bump in the road.

Haylee couldn't remember the last time she felt this kind of peace.

But it wasn't a fragile, fleeting kind. It was the kind of peace that came from acceptance—not the easy kind, where everything goes your way, but the kind you earn by walking through hard truths and still choosing to move forward. She'd faced pieces of her past she hadn't known were waiting for her. She'd embraced parts of herself she used to ignore. And now, she was choosing to live wide open.

She didn't have a destination in mind, but that didn't scare her anymore.

A few hours later, Haylee pulled into a roadside farmer's market just outside a small town. Bright tents flapped in the wind, and the scent of fresh bread and herbs filled the air. She turned off the engine and glanced in the rearview mirror.

"Snack stop, girls?" she asked with a grin.

Josie perked up immediately.

She wandered through the market, tasting peach slices and tiny samples of goat cheese, watching a local bluegrass trio strum their guitars in front of a battered produce truck. A vendor handed Haylee a jar of wildflower honey shaped like a bear, and Bella became an instant celebrity among a group of kids who asked to pet her.

There was something grounding about this place—real people, small joys, slow moments.

Haylee bought a few things: fresh strawberries, a loaf of cinnamon bread, a tiny bottle of lavender oil for the RV. As she tucked them away in her canvas tote, she caught sight of a local bulletin board near the exit. Paper flyers and handwritten signs advertised everything from lost pets to yoga classes and open mic nights.

One flyer, printed in faded blue ink, caught her eye:
"Writers' Circle – Every Wednesday at 6pm | The Hollow Bean Café | Share your story. Listen to others. Heal."

She tore off one of the tabs at the bottom before she could talk herself out of it.

Back at Bertha, as she pulled onto the road again, Haylee watched the mountains disappear in the side mirror. Ahead, the horizon was wide and waiting.

She hadn't journalled much in the past couple of days. Not because she didn't want to—but because she was sitting with everything she'd uncovered. Letting it sink in. But now, with the Writers' Circle flyer folded in her lap, she felt something stir.

Maybe it was time to speak a little louder.

She found a quiet campground just outside of town, tucked between a field of wildflowers and a narrow creek. That evening, as the sky painted itself in soft oranges and violets, Haylee opened her journal again.

This time, the words poured out effortlessly:

"Freedom isn't the absence of responsibility. It's the presence of truth. And when you live in your truth, you stop chasing approval and start chasing peace. For years, I thought I was running away. Now I know—I was always running toward something. Toward myself. Toward this life. Toward love, and loss, and all the messy, magical in-betweens. The road is both teacher and mirror. I'm not who I was when I left home. And I'm grateful for that."

The next day, she walked into the café.

It smelled of cinnamon and espresso. The kind of place with mismatched chairs and shelves lined with secondhand books. A small group was already gathered at a circle of tables in the back. Haylee's fingers fidgeted on the paper tab from the flyer, now worn soft in her palm.

Someone greeted her with a warm smile and a nod toward an empty chair. "Welcome. We're just getting started."

Haylee sat down. Her heart raced a little, but it wasn't fear. It was anticipation.

When her turn came, she opened her journal, hesitated for a heartbeat, then began to read. Her voice trembled at first, but grew steadier with each sentence. She talked about Aggie, about letting go, about finding joy in unexpected places. And when she looked up, she saw tears in a few eyes—and something else.

Connection.

After the circle ended, someone tapped her shoulder. A woman in her late forties, dressed in flannel and worn jeans.
"Your story," she said gently. "It reminded me why I started traveling again. After my divorce, I thought I was lost. But maybe we're not lost—we're just between places. Thank you."

That night, Haylee returned to Bertha with a quiet smile on her face.
The road ahead was still uncertain, but her voice had found its rhythm again.

Chapter 27:
The Pen in Her Hand

The road was wide open ahead, as if the universe itself had cleared a path just for Haylee. She had always imagined the future as a vast, uncharted territory, something to be feared or avoided, but now it felt like a canvas. The horizon stretched before her, endless and full of promise. There were no more limits, no more "shoulds" or "musts." There was just the present moment—and in this moment, Haylee knew she was ready to keep going.

It had become a ritual for Haylee—a time of quiet reflection, a moment just for herself. Every evening, as the sun dipped below the horizon and the sky turned to soft shades of purple and pink, she would pull out the small leather journal her aunt had once given her. The journal, much like Bertha, had seen its fair share of miles, and now it was the one constant in a life that was constantly in motion.

Haylee had started writing early on in her journey. At first, it was a way to process the overwhelming newness of living on the road, the freedom she had craved for so long. But now, as the months passed, the journal had become more than just a collection of thoughts. It had become her mirror, reflecting not just her experiences, but the growth that had come with each day.

June 22, 2024

It's funny how life can change in a blink of an eye. I thought I knew who I was back before I left, back when everything felt heavy, like I was carrying the weight of the world on my shoulders. But now, it feels lighter. Not easy, not always perfect, but lighter. More mine.

Today, I met a woman named Zoe who's been on the road for years. I think she's probably the most open-minded, confident person I've ever met. I envy her ability to move through the world without hesitation, but I'm starting to realize that maybe I've been doing the same thing, just in my own way. She gave me some great tips today, too—about staying safe as a solo traveler, how perception is key. I still have a lot to learn, but maybe that's the fun part.

I think of Aunt Aggie often, especially now.

This journey, in a way, is a tribute to her. I see it in the way I journal, the way I navigate my days. Aunt Aggie would've loved seeing me in this RV, just like she did when I was a kid, telling me that the world is so much bigger than what we think we know. She was a woman who knew how to live fully, even when things weren't perfect. I wish I had listened more back then.

But I'm listening now. To the road, to myself, and to the people I meet along the way.

Haylee closed the journal, her heart heavy with the realization that her aunt's spirit was still with her, guiding her. In many ways, Haylee was becoming the woman she had always admired in her aunt. Not just in the way she had lived her life, but in the way she had documented it—through words, through reflection, through a quiet understanding that every step, every misstep, was part of the larger journey.

She set the journal down beside her and leaned back against the RV, letting the stillness of the night wash over her. The sounds of crickets, the soft rustling of leaves, and the occasional laughter from other campers filled the air. In that moment, Haylee realized just how far she had come from the woman she had been only a few months ago. Her journey wasn't just about traveling—it was about learning who she was meant to be, and finding the strength to move forward with each passing day.

Reflection and Action

As days and weeks passed, Haylee's journaling became more than just a nightly routine. It was a way of marking her progress, of capturing the lessons she learned and the feelings she often couldn't express out loud. With every entry, she grew more connected to the woman she was becoming—stronger, braver, more sure of herself.

And it wasn't just the adventures or the tips from other travelers that shaped her; it was the quiet moments of reflection—the times when she took a step back and realized just how much she had changed.

One evening, a few weeks after the rally, she sat by a campfire with Josie and Bella beside her, the flames casting a warm glow across her face. Haylee pulled out her journal and wrote:

August 12, 2024

I don't think I would have been ready for this journey if I hadn't started journaling, at least not in the way I am now. I read through some of my early entries today, and it's wild to see how much I've grown. I've met so many amazing people on the road, and every one of them has helped me become more of who I'm meant to be.

But it's the quiet times, the moments when I'm alone with my thoughts, that make all of this worth it. Aunt Aggie used to say that "The road always gives you what you need, even when you don't know you need it."

She was right. Every day on this journey, I find pieces of myself I never knew existed. And with each step, I'm more sure of where I'm headed. For the first time, I'm not afraid of what's coming next.

Haylee closed the journal, a sense of calm settling over her. She had been on the road for a while now, but this felt like the beginning. The beginning of a life she had crafted with her own hands, a life that was truly her own.

As the weeks unfolded, Haylee's journaling deepened her understanding of herself.

She'd started this journey seeking answers to questions she didn't even know how to ask, but with every entry in her journal, more pieces of the puzzle came together. What had begun as a means of processing her emotions and fears had blossomed into something much more meaningful—a mirror to reflect back her growth, her desires, and even her fears.

One evening, as she sat by the fire, the warmth from the flames chasing away the cool evening air, she found herself lost in thought. Josie was sprawled out beside her, lazily chewing on a stick she'd found earlier in the day, while Bella sat perched on the dashboard, watching the flickering light outside the RV. Haylee pulled out her journal, the familiar leather cover still worn and soft from months of use, and began to write.

October 25, 2024

I've been on the road for almost six months now, and I'm starting to feel like this life is mine—not something I'm trying to force into being, but something I've made. It's funny, but for the first time in a long time, I don't feel like I'm missing anything.

Aunt Aggie's words echo in my mind more than I'd like to admit. She used to say that the world always gives you what you need, even if you don't recognize it at the time. I thought she was being poetic or idealistic, but I see now that she was right. This journey has shown me that I am the one who needs to change. The road didn't need to change me—it was always inside me, waiting to be uncovered.

Sometimes, it's hard not to fall back into old patterns of doubt. The road can be lonely, and my mind tends to wander to the people I've left behind, the life I used to have. But when I sit down and think about it, I realize that I wasn't living before —I was existing.

This—what I'm doing now—this is life. Even the mistakes, the unplanned detours, the breakdowns, the late-night fears. It's all part of it.

Haylee closed her journal, a small sigh of contentment escaping her lips.

Her life felt like a patchwork quilt, woven together with a thousand different threads—some frayed, some strong, some in places she never would have imagined. But they all contributed to the whole, and now, for the first time in ages, she understood that this patchwork was exactly what she needed.

The campfire crackled softly in the night, its flames casting a warm glow across Haylee's face. The sky had darkened to a deep shade of indigo, with stars twinkling like scattered diamonds. Josie, as usual, lay at her feet, paws twitching occasionally as she dreamt, and Bella was perched comfortably on the driver's seat inside Bertha, looking out the window at the quiet evening.

Haylee's fingers lightly traced the edges of her journal as she sat back against the RV. It had become her refuge—her place to process, to reflect, and, most importantly, to give voice to the parts of her that hadn't fully healed. She'd read through her past entries and felt how much had changed, but the overwhelming emotion now was gratitude, tinged with awe at how far she'd come.

She opened the journal to a fresh page, feeling the cool evening breeze against her skin, and wrote:

November 01, 2024

I've been reflecting a lot lately, especially as I sit here watching the fire dance. It's such a contrast to what I was used to—sitting in my small house, the hum of traffic just outside, the constant buzz of technology demanding my attention. There was always noise back then. Now, the quiet feels more like a friend than a stranger.

In the past, I would've felt lonely out here. Alone in the wilderness, miles away from anything familiar. But somehow, the more I step into this new life, the less I feel the need to be tethered to anything or anyone.
I don't know if I'm ready to say goodbye to everything from my past yet, but I'm certainly not trying to hold on anymore. And that feels good.

It's not always easy, though. It's easy to get lost in the idea of being alone. There are moments when I feel like I'm missing something—someone—but then I look around at the world I'm creating, and I realize that everything I need is here.

Josie, Bella, the freedom, the open road, and the people I've met. These are the things that fill me up now.

I've also realized that I've been running for a long time, but not away from people. It's been about running away from myself—away from fear, away from failure, faway rom the voice that kept telling me I wasn't good enough. The funny thing is, I never would've thought running would help. But it's the most honest thing I've ever done. It's the only thing that's made sense.

I'm running toward myself. And that makes all the difference.

Haylee paused after writing those words, feeling the weight of them settle over her like a soft blanket. She glanced over at Josie, who was now resting her head on her paws, and Bella, who had curled up tighter in the driver's seat.

"I think I finally understand what Aunt Aggie meant," Haylee murmured aloud, almost as though speaking to the stars. "The road always gives you what you need —even when you don't know you need it."

A sense of calm enveloped her as she closed the journal. She hadn't just come to this place physically—she had come to it emotionally, too. In the distance, she saw the first signs of dawn approaching, the first tendrils of light breaking through the horizon, and she felt a deep sense of connection to everything around her.

The road had given her something she hadn't even known to ask for—herself.

Watch for Signs

Haylee decided to go for a walk to clear her mind. The air was crisp, the kind of coolness that made her feel alive, and she had Josie by her side as usual. But as they ventured farther from the RV park, Haylee had a strange feeling. A gut instinct that something was off.

She stopped in her tracks, feeling a tension rise in the pit of her stomach. There were a couple of men near the edge of the park, standing by a rundown truck. They had been there when she first arrived, but she hadn't thought much of them at the time. Now, as the minutes passed, she felt an unsettling chill crawl up her spine.

Josie growled softly, a low, warning rumble.

Haylee's mind raced. She had been taught to trust her instincts, and right now, every fiber of her being screamed that she needed to leave. Without thinking twice, she turned and began walking briskly back toward the RV park, keeping her pace steady, not showing any sign of panic. Josie kept close by her side, alert to any movement.

As they neared the park, Haylee felt the men's eyes on her, but she didn't look back. Her hand instinctively went to the key fob in her pocket. If she had to make a quick getaway, she would be ready. She reached the RV and locked the door behind her, breathing a sigh of relief as the tension in her body began to ease.

Once inside, she let herself relax for a moment, glancing out the window to make sure no one was following her. Josie jumped onto the couch beside her, curling up into a ball, and Bella meowed from the front.

"That was close, huh, girl?" Haylee whispered, her fingers brushing the top of Josie's head. She had learned an important lesson: sometimes, the road wasn't just about the beautiful sunsets and serene landscapes—it was about staying alert, listening to her intuition, and trusting herself in those moments of uncertainty.

As the evening drew near, Haylee sat down with her journal again, feeling a renewed sense of clarity.

November 01, 2024

The road doesn't always give you what you expect—but it always gives you what you need. Today, it gave me a reminder to listen to myself and trust the signs around me. It's easy to get caught up in the excitement of new places and new faces, but I can't forget that the journey is not just about the beauty—it's about staying grounded, staying safe, and always trusting my gut.

Tonight, I feel stronger. Ready for whatever comes next.

With that final thought, Haylee closed her journal and leaned back, allowing the peace of the evening to settle over her. The world was full of unknowns, but for the first time, she felt ready to face whatever came her way.

Chapter 28:
RV Life Mishaps

Since that pivotal stretch of road, she had thrown herself into journaling with new intention, setting aside sacred time each morning to write. She even began posting short videos about her journey—not for likes or validation, but as a way of owning her story. And for the first time, she was doing it entirely on her own terms.

The response surprised her. Encouraging comments began to roll in—strangers cheering her on, thanking her for her honesty, and sharing their own stories in return. There was no pressure to explain herself anymore. No need to prove that she was "doing it right." She simply was. And that was enough.

Each day, she woke with a sense of quiet confidence, a steadier outlook. Not every day was smooth—there were still setbacks and frustrations—but her reaction to them had changed. When the generator wouldn't start or something broke unexpectedly, she no longer spiraled into doubt. She gave herself permission to pause, take a breath, and try again. She was learning not just how to live on the road, but how to live with herself.

Still, self-doubt crept in now and then. Sometimes she'd stare at the screen, hovering over the upload button, wondering who she thought she was to share her journey in a world already crowded with influencers and storytellers. What made her voice worth hearing?

One afternoon, while cleaning the solar panels on Bertha's roof, she nearly slipped and tumbled off the edge. Shaken but unharmed, she sat there afterward, laughing at the absurdity of it all. That evening, still chuckling at her own clumsiness, she opened her laptop and created a new video: "The Mishaps of RV Life." She uploaded it with a shrug, unsure how it would be received.

To her surprise, the response was instant and warm. Laughing emojis, shared stories of similar mishaps, tips from seasoned RVers—it wasn't just a video; it was a conversation. She had tapped into something real. It wasn't about being polished—it was about being honest.

And then, something unexpected happened.

173

This Time, Opportunity Texted

Sitting in Bertha, the sun low and golden on the horizon, Haylee's phone buzzed with a message that made her sit up straight.

"Hey Haylee, hope all's well. I came across your videos and loved your perspective. Would you be interested in submitting a piece for our travel magazine? We're looking for fresh voices, and I think your story could really resonate."

She blinked at the message, heart thudding. A magazine? Someone wanted her stor y?
Her fingers trembled as she replied.

"I'd love to. Thank you so much for reaching out. I'll send something soon."

She set the phone down and exhaled slowly, absorbing the moment. It didn't mean she had everything figured out—but maybe she didn't need to. She just had to keep showing up.

White Space and Stalled Thoughts

That evening, with the soft symphony of crickets outside and a cool breeze whispering through the open window, Haylee sat at her tiny desk in Bertha. Her laptop glowed before her, waiting. The cursor blinked on an empty page.

The words didn't come easily at first. Doubt hovered close. What could she possibly say that hadn't already been said?

Then she thought of how far she'd come—from losing her job and her house, to leaving behind a toxic relationship and a version of herself that had grown too small. She thought of the heartbreak, the fear, and how that chaos had somehow shaped this new version of her. One built not on certainty, but on courage.

And so she wrote.

Paragraph by paragraph, the piece came together. It was raw, vulnerable, and imperfect—but it was hers. When she finished, she reread it with a mix of pride and nerves, then hit send.

Haylee looked up to find Josie stretched out on the couch beside Bella, who had curled into a tight, purring ball. She smiled. "Alright, girl," she said, grabbing Josie's leash, "let's go."

As they walked beneath a streaky pink-and-indigo sky, Haylee felt a strange mix of exhilaration and fear settle in her chest. What had I just done? she wondered. She'd poured her story—her real story—into that piece and sent it off to someone she'd never met.

But then she remembered: they reached out to me. They saw something in her already.

Held Breath

The next few days passed in a blur of nervous anticipation. Haylee kept busy—filming new videos, editing, walking Josie, exploring roadside diners and talking to locals. She posted another "RV bloopers" clip and laughed at the growing comment thread of shared chaos. Yet, in the quiet moments, she couldn't help wondering:

What if the magazine hated it? What if I'm not good enough?

But even those thoughts couldn't take away the truth of what she'd done. She had shown up. That mattered.

A week later, as she sat sipping coffee outside Bertha in the early morning light, her phone buzzed again.

"Haylee, we loved your submission. We'd be honored to feature it in our next issue.

Let's talk details."
For a few seconds, she just stared at the screen. Then she jumped to her feet with a squeal of disbelief. Josie barked in surprise, tail wagging furiously.

"We did it," Haylee whispered, grinning so wide it hurt. "We really did it."

She wasn't chasing someone else's idea of success anymore. She wasn't waiting for permission. She had told her story, and the world had listened.

And in that moment, with the wind in her hair and the wide open road still stretching before her, Haylee knew—this was only the beginning.

Title: Off the Map: How I Found Myself on the Road
By Haylee Hensen

When I first hit the road in my aging RV (lovingly named Bertha), I didn't do it for the freedom, the views, or some lifelong dream of RV life. I did it because everything else in my life had fallen apart. I had lost my job. My relationship ended. I sold my house. And somewhere along the way, I had lost my sense of self, too. What began as a desperate move became something else entirely—a return to myself.

At first, it was chaos. I didn't know how to fix a fuse or troubleshoot a water pump. I cried when the generator refused to turn over in the middle of a rainstorm. I panicked when I took a wrong turn and ended up on a backroad with no cell service. But I figured it out, little by little. The road, as it turns out, has a way of teaching you things you didn't know you needed to learn.

People think traveling alone must be lonely, but I've never felt more connected. I've shared stories with strangers around campfires. I've gotten directions from gas station clerks who treated me like family. I've laughed with fellow RVers about the endless mishaps—because trust me, there are plenty. (Like the time I almost slid off the roof cleaning my solar panels. Lesson learned: dry boots, always.)

I started posting videos mostly for fun, capturing the quiet in-between moments— the kind of things that don't make travel brochures: breakdowns, detours, spilled coffee, wrong turns. I thought no one would care. But to my surprise, people did. They wrote back. They saw themselves in the messiness. And I realized that maybe the beauty of this life isn't just in the mountaintop views, but in the resilience it takes to climb the hill in the first place.

Traveling solo taught me to trust my instincts again. It taught me that solitude can be sacred, and that being "lost" doesn't always mean something is wrong. Sometimes it means you're exactly where you're supposed to be.

My journey hasn't been perfect, but it's been real. And if there's one thing I've learned out here, it's this: You don't have to have all the answers. You just have to be willing to take the next step—even if you're not sure where the road leads. Because sometimes, off the map is where the real story begins.

Editor's Note

We first came across Haylee Jensen through a late-night rabbit hole of RV travel videos. Among glossy drone shots and curated itineraries, her voice stood out—raw, real, and quietly powerful. Haylee doesn't just document places; she shares the soul of the road and the healing that can happen when life breaks apart and you choose to move forward anyway. Her story is a reminder that courage doesn't always roar. Sometimes it rolls up slowly, engine humming, with a rescue dog in the passenger seat and a whole lot of heart. We're honored to feature her in this issue of Roam Free.

— Natalie Cruz, Editor-in-Chief

Chapter 29:
A Whisper From the Past

As twilight crept in and the desert turned to shadows, Haylee's phone buzzed in her back pocket.

Unknown number.

She paused, pulling it out. One new message.

"They're not who you think. Aggie lied to protect you. Look into Elliot. Ask your father what really happened the year before she left."

Haylee's breath caught.

Not again.

Her fingers hovered over the screen, heart pounding. She hadn't received one of these messages in weeks—not since the mountains. She had convinced herself it was someone playing games. Maybe someone from Aggie's past. Maybe a troll. But this? This was too specific.

She glanced over at Josie, her faithful companion sniffing at a cactus bloom, completely unaware that the world had just tilted beneath Haylee's feet again.

Who was Elliot? Why would Aggie lie about anything—especially to her?

That last line… "Ask your father what really happened…"

Haylee turned cold. She had asked him about Aggie before. He had brushed her off, saying Agnes was a "free spirit," that things had just drifted apart. Nothing suspicious. But now—she had been warned.

She opened her contacts, thumb hovering over "Dad."

No. Not yet. Not like this.

Instead, she screenshotted the message and forwarded it to him with a note: "Dad, I just got this. Again. You told me everything… didn't you?"

She stared at the screen, but no bubbles appeared. No reply. Just a sinking feeling in her gut.

The Message and the Silence

The desert evening had cooled, and the stars were beginning to appear when Haylee sent the screenshot to her dad. She waited, phone in hand, heart pacing in time with Josie's panting. But there was no reply. Not that night.

She didn't sleep well.

Even inside the safety of Bertha, with the doors locked and Josie curled at her feet, she couldn't shake the feeling that someone was watching her. Every creak of the RV felt suspicious. Every gust of wind against the side made her nerves jolt. The message kept looping in her mind.

They're not who you think. Aggie lied to protect you. Look into Elliot.

She opened the message again. No profile picture. No name. No metadata that gave anything away. The number was untraceable.

By morning, her eyes were gritty from lack of sleep. She went through the motions —coffee, journaling, brushing down Josie—but her thoughts were elsewhere.

When the reply finally came in around 9:13 a.m., it was maddeningly short.

Dad: "We'll talk soon. Not over text."

That was it.

No "don't worry."

No "it's nothing."

No "I don't know who Elliot is."

Just avoidance.

Haylee stared at the message for a long time, her stomach flipping. Her dad had always been direct, especially after Aggie died. But this? This was careful. Strategic. Which meant he knew something.

And now the bigger question was gnawing at her: how did the mystery texter know where to reach her?

Her number wasn't public. She hadn't posted it anywhere. The only place she'd shared any part of her life was YouTube—and even that, she'd been careful about. No last names. No specific locations until after she'd left them.

Still… someone could be watching. Someone was watching.

She opened her channel and clicked through the comments. Most were friendly, even goofy—people sharing tips about the RV mishaps, folks telling her how brave she was. But now she read them with a different lens. Every vague username. Every emoji-laden compliment.

Was it them?

Were they trying to scare her off the road? Or was this a warning?

She closed her laptop and stood up quickly, her heart racing. She pulled back the curtain and peeked out the small window above the kitchenette. Just a couple of other RVs nearby. A family setting up a grill. An older man walking his dog. Nothing unusual.

But still… something felt off.

Haylee scribbled a line in her journal before she forgot the thought:

"If someone knows where I am, why haven't they approached me? What are they waiting for?

Threads in the Dark

Over the next few days, Haylee tried to shake the feeling that someone was watching her—but the signs kept piling up. It started innocently enough. A new comment on one of her latest videos, where she had filmed a time-lapse of the sunrise through Bertha's front window, caught
her attention:
"That coffee mug on your dash... Aggie always loved those bold colors. She used to say it reminded her of Santa Fe."
Haylee blinked at the screen.
She hadn't said anything about the mug. Not in the video, not in the caption. She hadn't even noticed it was in the shot. But someone had. And more than that—someone knew it belonged to Aggie.
She clicked on the profile: no uploads, no subscriber count, no bio. Just a username: ElliotRoad12.
Her stomach dropped.
She didn't know anyone named Elliot. At least... she didn't think she did.
Haylee sat back slowly, her skin prickling with the unmistakable weight of being seen too closely. Whoever this was—this Elliot—they weren't just watching. They knew things. Personal things. Things only someone close to Aggie, or her dad, might have known.
Later that afternoon, she pulled into a rest stop off a quiet stretch of highway in New Mexico. Just a short break to stretch her legs and let Josie out. She was tired, distracted, her thoughts looping around questions with no answers.
When she returned to the RV, something fluttering under the windshield wiper caught her eye.
It was a note.
Her breath caught as she pulled it free, the paper slightly damp from morning dew. The handwriting was quick, almost rushed.
"Aggie never told you everything."
Haylee stood there, frozen, the note trembling in her fingers. The wind shifted, warm and dry, but it did nothing to thaw the ice in her veins. She scanned the rest area—an older couple packing up a picnic, a trucker stepping out to smoke, a mom wrangling her toddler near the vending machines. No one looked suspicious. No one seemed to be watching her.
But someone had been close enough to leave this.

Haylee: Dad. Someone left a note on my RV. It said "Aggie never told you everything." Please. I need to know who Elliot is. You said we'd talk. This can't wait anymore.

She watched the screen for minutes. No response.

An hour passed.

Then two.

Finally, just as she was about to give up and call, her phone buzzed with a reply.

Dad: "Not over text. We'll talk soon. I promise."

She threw her phone on the bed, frustration rising. Why couldn't he just tell her? That night, Haylee opened Aggie's old journals again—the ones she hadn't looked at in months, tucked away in the trunk under her bed. She flipped through the pages, scanning for any mention of "Elliot."

Halfway through a worn leather-bound book dated 1996, she found a reference that made her go still.

"Saw Elliot again today. It's strange seeing him with David after everything that happened. I still don't think Haylee should ever know."

David. Her dad.

Haylee's heart pounded.

Who was Elliot? What happened between the three of them? And why was Aggie so determined to keep it from her?

Haylee closed Aggie's journal slowly, her fingers brushing the ink like it might burn her. Outside, the desert night pressed in on Bertha, silent but full of whispers.

She didn't know what she was walking into.

But she wasn't turning back.

About the Author

Kimber Guise is the author of Keys to Wonderlust, a story inspired by her own nomadic lifestyle. She is a full-time traveler, adventurer, and storyteller who explores the open roads of North America in her beloved RV. Accompanied by her loyal pup and curious cats, she embraces a nomadic lifestyle rich with discovery, quiet moments, and scenic detours. From winding mountain passes to tucked-away campgrounds, Kimber finds inspiration in the natural beauty of National and State Parks across the United States and Canada. A published author and lifelong reader, Kimber believes stories have the power to connect us, heal us, and remind us who we are. When she's not writing, you'll find her chasing sunsets, sipping coffee by a campfire, or browsing the shelves of a local bookstore. She's committed to savoring the journey—wherever the road may lead. Follow Kimber's adventures and writing life on TikTok and Instagram **@vibing.rvlife**, on Facebook at **Vibing RV Life**, or on YouTube under **Kimber Guise (@vibing.rvlife)**.

The key is always with her.

www.ingramcontent.com/pod-product-compliance
Lightning Source LLC
Chambersburg PA
CBHW070311040726
47501CB00019B/2232